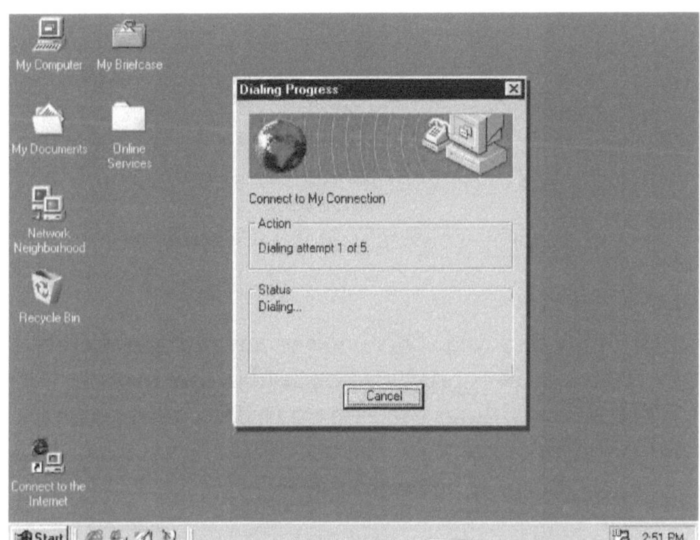

My Computer
My Briefcase
My Documents
Online Services
Network Neighborhood
Recycle Bin
Connect to the Internet
Dialing Progress
Connect to My Connection
Action
Dialing attempt 1 of 5.
Status
Dialing...
Cancel
Start
2:51 PM

AF368504

Dial-Up and Die

By P. J. Thorndyke

2024 by Copyright © P. J. Thorndyke

"With all the media focus on the online safety of our youth in the post-social media age, it seems somewhat redundant to look at those early days of the internet through the same lens. It seems to us now as little more than a quaint age of diul-up modems, chatrooms and fan sites. But in the case of the Montgomery County Murders of 1999, the warning signs were there all along ..." – Ghost in the Machine: The Montgomery County Murders by David Williamson

ICQ History Log (05/20/99)

Started on Thu May 20 21:34:25 1999

Participants:

Casey Jackson – Casey

Philip Cox – Phil/C

Frederick Bronson - FreddiesFingers

Riley Parker - PrincessKirigoe

PrincessKirigoe – Hello? Anybody there?!?!

FreddiesFingers – Freddie's Fingers in da house!

Phil/C – YO!!!!!!

PrincessKirigoe – Where's Casey?

FreddiesFingers – Late as usual.

PrincessKirigoe – She's been acting weird lately. I can't be the only one whose noticed?

FreddiesFingers – We've noticed. What's going on with her, Phil?

Phil/C – How the hell should I know?

FreddiesFingers – She's your fucking girlfriend.

Phil/C – Doesn't mean I can read her mind. She's been real distant lately.

PrincessKirigoe – Has anybody heard anything about that contest? It's been almost a month since we submitted our stories.

FreddiesFingers – I bet we all got gypped and somebody is gonna rip off our stories without paying us.

PrincessKirigoe – That WAS a legit site, right, Phil?

Phil/C – Yeah, of course it was. But, um … the site seems to be gone. ¯_(")_/¯

FreddiesFingers – What do you mean GONE?

Phil/C – Just gone. Not there anymore.

FreddiesFingers – Man, we definitely got ripped off.

PrincessKirigoe – Phil, I put so much effort into that story!

Phil/C – Hey, so did I! It's not my fault.

PrincessKirigoe – Well, Casey's gonna be crushed. She really got into it.

Phil/C – Fuck it. I don't even care anymore. So, Freddie, you have any more cybersex with this online babe of yours?

FreddiesFingers – A gentleman never tells.

Phil/C – Correct. So, any more cybersex?

PrincessKirigoe – Hahaha! Freddy's no gentleman! Spill, Freddie!

FreddiesFingers – Screw you guys

PrincessKirigoe – I'm not convinced this girlfriend of yours isn't inflatable. I seem to remember you have a history with those types of ladies? ;-)

Phil/C – Oh, yeah! Old Doris! I forgot about her!

FreddiesFingers – Fuck you both. At least I do something more productive with my time than play dumb online games. Speaking of which, are you two any closer to cracking the case?

PrincessKirigoe – We solved the latest puzzle. You were right, none of those shorts in the video were from a horror movie.

FreddiesFingers – Somebody wanted them to look like Cronenberg but a horror aficionado like me can spot an amateur. You still think it's some NSA or FBI recruitment process?

PrincessKirigoe – Gotta be.

FreddiesFingers – Haha! It's so obviously a game, Riley. You think the Feds would waste time with online riddles? Either that or someone's just fucking with you.

PrincessKirigoe – You won't be laughing when we're part of a government training program come next spring.

FreddiesFingers – You might be but Phil is too much of a dumb shit to join any government organization ;-p

Phil/C – Fuck you Freddie

FreddiesFingers – How does Casey feel about you guys playing Nancy Drew together?

Phil/C – She's fine with it.

Casey – You're right. I'm fine with it.

FreddiesFingers – Speak of the devil!

PrincessKirigoe – Caaaasseyyyy!!!! Took you long enough to join!

Casey – I was a little tied up.

PrincessKirigoe – Um, Casey, did you read about the story competition above?

Casey – Yeah. It's cool. I'd kind of forgotten about the story contest anyway.

FreddiesFingers – How about we have our own little contest right here? Three sentence horror stories. Best one wins.

PrincessKirigoe – OK, Freddie. You go first.

FreddiesFingers – Shucks, may I? All right then.

FreddiesFingers – A little girl gets a Barbie doll for Christmas. She asks her mom why there is no such thing as a pregnant Barbie doll. Her mom replies: "Because Ken always comes in another box."

PrincessKirigoe – Freddieeeeeee!!!! That wasn't even a horror story!

Phil/C – And you totally stole it. I read that one online.

FreddiesFingers – I didn't say they had to be original stories.

PrincessKirigoe – OK, me! People say my house is haunted. They're frightened to come inside. I think it's bullshit because I've lived here for 342 years and I've never seen a single ghost.

FreddiesFingers – Haha! Good one! Phil, you're up!

Phil/C – A girl meets a boy online and they fall in love (see where this is going, Freddie?). They have lots of cybersex, real dirty stuff, but after a while, the girl decides she wants to speak to the boy in person. She looks up his phone number and gives it a call ... and her dad picks up ...

PrincessKirigoe – Gross!

FreddiesFingers – That was technically four sentences.

Phil/C – Well you can technically suck my dick.

PrincessKirigoe – Haha! We'll allow it because it was a good story, Phil. Casey's turn!

Phil/C – Yo, Casey. You there?

Casey – Yeah, I just had to check something. Noises outside.

PrincessKirigoe – Your parents home?

Casey – No. They've gone to watch Bobby's basketball match. I'm home alone.

Phil/C – What kind of noises?

Casey – It sounded like somebody moving around on the patio. It's stopped now.

Phil/C – Your turn, Casey. The best three sentence horror story you can think of. Go!

Casey – Ummmm, I don't really know if I can …

PrincessKirigoe – Sure you can.

Phil/C – Didn't you tell me you wrote a killer short story for the contest?

PrincessKirigoe – Too bad no one's every going to read it, Phil.

Phil/C – Not my fault. How many times do I have to say it?

Casey – Guys, I'm starting to get a little freaked out now. The noises are back and when I looked out the window, I think I saw a shadow move behind the bushes.

Phil/C – Are your doors locked?

Casey – I'm going to check them now.

Casey – I'm back and I'm seriously scared guys. I locked all the doors and before I came back upstairs, I looked through the peephole. I'm pretty sure a man is standing on our porch, just out of sight.

PrincessKirigoe – Are you sure?

Casey – Yes, I'm sure, Riley! I saw him!

PrincessKirigoe – Ok, just stay to stay calm. If the doors are locked then there's nothing he can do, right?

Phil/C – Call the cops.

Casey – I don't want to log off. I need to keep talking to you guys. I don't want to be alone.

PrincessKirigoe – Ummm, where's Freddie? He's been inactive for a while now...

Phil/C – Oh, man! It's Freddie. He's fucking with you!

Casey – Freddie, is this you?

Phil/C – Answer the question, Freddie. This you?

PrincessKirigoe – Joke's over, Freddie. Quit it.

Casey – Shit! He's hammering on the door!

PrincessKirigoe – I don't think it's Freddie. You should log off and call the cops.

Casey – OK. I'm gonna call them.

Phil/C – As soon as you do, get back on here and keep us updated.

Phil/C – Casey?

PrincessKirigoe – She's still showing as online.

Casey – It doesn't work! I pulled out the phone line and I'm still online! I can't call anybody!

Phil/C – Casey, that's impossible.

PrincessKirigoe – Are you messing with us, Casey?

Casey – I swear I'm not messing with you. Who's doing this?????

Phil/C – Freddie I swear to God if this is you I will kill you!!!

PrincessKirigoe – Is the man still outside?

Casey – I don't know. I can't hear him. I'm too scared to go check.

Casey – I heard a noise on this side of the house! It's like he's all around me!

Casey – I think he's trying to get in

Phil/C – Casey?

PrincessKirigoe – Casey, where are you?!?!?!?! Answer us please!!!!

FreddiesFingers – Hey guys. What's up? My mom wanted to use the phone.

Phil/C – Are you fukn kidding me?

FreddiesFingers – What?

PrincessKirigoe – Freddie, read our chat log.

FreddiesFingers – Holy shit. What's going on over there?

Phil/C – You tell us.

FreddiesFingers – I've no fucking idea. It's not me!

Phil/C – What were you doing when you were offline?

FreddiesFingers – Nothing!

FreddiesFingers – Just chilling in my room, I swear!

PrincessKirigoe – This has gone too far. I don't care if it's a joke, I'm calling the cops.

NEWS ARTICLE FROM THE MONTGOMERY COUNTY SENTINEL, (05/21/99)

TRAGIC DEATH OF HIGH SCHOOL BEAUTY BAFFLES POLICE

The body of 18-year-old Casey Jackson was found last night not far from her home in a patch of scrubland near Randolph Road. The cause of death was determined to have been heart failure.

Casey had been home alone and chatted to friends online at around 21:30 p.m. when her friends began to notice her erratic behavior. She seemed increasingly concerned that somebody had either broken into her house or was attempting to do so. Her friends advised her to call the police though there is no record that any such call was made from her house.

It is estimated that Casey left her house around 21:50 p.m. in a distressed state and wearing nothing but her underwear and a white Tasmanian Devil t-shirt. It was at this point that one of her friends called the police and a unit was dispatched to the neighborhood of Connecticut Avenue Estates.

A couple walking their dog reported seeing Casey heading north towards Wakefield High School. She seemed concerned that somebody was pursuing her as she kept looking back over her shoulder. The couple said that they saw nobody behind her. Police found her body at around 22:30 in a wooded area below the county highway. She had been unmolested and appeared to have had a heart attack. After an investigation of her house, police could detect no sign of any break-in.

Casey Jackson was a well-liked student at Wakefield High. She was on the lacrosse team and was a high achiever with straight As. According to friends, her behavior over the weeks leading up to her death was increasingly strange. Concerns about drug use which could have affected her psychological state as well as contributing to her death have not been confirmed.

BEAUTY IN DARKNESS: THE ONLINE JOURNAL OF CHLOE EVANS (05/21/99)

These entries originally appeared on a website hosted by Angelfire which was taken down in late 1999. Copies of the posts were made by persons unknown and began to appear on the 4chan imageboard website in 2015. They have since been verified as genuine.

May 21, 1999

Today a friend of mine died. Well, maybe 'friend' is a little generous. We didn't exactly hang out together anymore. We used to. We were friends in middle school, but I guess we kinda grew apart over the years. I mean, pick a pair of teenage girls who are as far apart as possible with regard to fashion, music, movie tastes and general attitude to life and you'll get something like us.

We used to hang out all the time. Casey arrived in fifth grade, and we instantly hit it off as she needed a friend and I didn't exactly have a whole lot of friends either. We hung out at each other's houses, had sleepovers in her treehouse and her parents kind of began to feel like my own, especially after my mom died. Dad didn't mind. I think he was just glad that I had somewhere to be while he dealt with his own grief. And that's why it hurt so much when Casey and I fell out.

I guess we were just too different in the end. Casey was a bright star. A popular girl, pretty and kind. Everybody liked her. Everybody thought she was sweet. And me? Well, you know all about me, don't you, my sweet darlings? (sinister laugh)

Ugh. Even being funny is a massive effort right now. I just can't do it, so I guess I'll tell you about Casey and what happened today.

She was found late last night in a crappy wooded area not far from our school wearing only her nightie. What she was doing there is the big mystery, matched only by how she died. The cops are saying heart attack. Yeah, right. I'm not sold on that. She was on the lacrosse team and was a hell of a lot healthier than I am. I smoke almost a pack of cloves a day so if anybody should be getting heart attacks, then it should be me.

Drugs have also been mentioned. Now, I may not have spoken to Casey much in the past five years, and I know she was hanging out with some sketchy dudes like her loser boyfriend Phil and his demented sidekick, Freddie, but I know for a fact that she would not get mixed up in drugs. She was too squeaky-clean for that. So no sale on the drugs angle.

So what the hell happened to her? She just sort of *dropped dead* and that's what's so weird about the whole thing. Why was she wandering out on her own in her PJs? There's something more to this and I have a feeling her little circle of douchebag friends know more than they're letting on. Everyone knows that Casey was talking to them online last night just before she left her house and wound up dead. The police were all over the school today, asking everybody questions. That none of them have been arrested yet means that they have a cover story sewn up pretty tight. If I find out that this was some dumb hazing thing or that they were picking on her or some shit like that ... they will know my fury like the wrath of an avenging angel. Casey might not have been my friend anymore, but she was a nice girl. *Too* nice for those guys.

Well, that's about it. I don't feel much like writing any more. This whole thing has me seriously bummed. I might write more tomorrow.

\m/ Stay dark and beautiful, gothlings.

Chloe

P.S. Despite the serious downer I'm on, I should probably tell you about that date I bigged up so much in my last entry. Suffice to say, there won't be a second date. He was OK, but not a good match. To start with, he's a wiccan and right off the bat, just assumed I was too. He started talking about Beltane and the upcoming equinox as if I was going to be dancing ass naked in the moonlight alongside him. I really hate it when people think I'm a wiccan just because I'm a goth. I despise that neopaganism shit. I guess I'll just stay lonely for a while. And with all that's happening now (see above), I really don't feel like company.

EMAIL FROM RILEY PARKER TO PHILIP COX (05/21/99)

Date: 05/21/1999

Time: 19:22

From: Riley Parker

To: Philip Cox

Subject: Re: Booooo! Scared ya!

Hey.

You're not online so I guess you're still talking to the cops or your parents or whatever. But I really need to talk to you so I'm sending you this. Promise you'll reply as soon as you read it? I'll be on ICQ all evening, so maybe we can chat?

I'm so fucked up over this whole thing. I just can't believe we were talking to Casey minutes before she … well. I don't even want to write it. I'm sorry. I know this must be harder on you than on anyone and here I am feeling sorry for myself. Are you OK? Please let me know.

Do you still think it was Freddie? I just can't see him doing something like that. I've known him all my life. He's been acting weird lately, but I can't see him as a murderer. Anyway, didn't they say that she died of a heart attack or something? There's no evidence that anybody did anything to her but still, a healthy girl like Casey dying of a heart attack? I don't get it. I mean, she was acting pretty weird the last few weeks … I just don't know what's going on.

Was there any chance that she knew about us?

Riley xoxo

PROFILE OF CASEY JACKSON

From *Ghost in the Machine: The Montgomery County Murders* by David Williamson (Tulane University Press: 2001), p. 34:

At a glance, the bedroom of Casey Jackson seems typical of an eighteen-year-old, middle class American girl. On the sloped ceiling, the boyish good looks of Ryan Gosling and Leonardo Di Caprio gaze down from a multitude of posters ripped from the pages of magazines. A corner desk supports a computer, a teenager's window into the limitless world of the web. Bottles of nail varnish surround a switched-off lava lamp, its congealed wax dull and cold. A wallet of CDs on top of the stereo contains albums by alternative rock bands like Red Hot Chili Peppers, Foo Fighters and Goo Goo Dolls. Nothing too heavy but with enough of an edge to suggest a certain level of youthful rebellion.

But look closer. The wallpaper peeking between the faces of the current teen heartthrobs of the day is a pastel pink, worn and faded, a relic from childhood, and there are teddy bears on a high shelf, just out of reach but still present, as if their owner has outgrown them but can't bring herself to banish them to the attic or garage. Casey's room is a confluence of childish innocence and adolescent awakening emblematic of those on the cusp of adulthood.

That Casey Jackson never got to enjoy that adulthood is one of the tragedies of our age. Her room has been kept as it is by her parents. Aside from the inevitable disturbance by the police as they poked through Casey's belongings looking for answers, the room remains as she left it that warm May evening in 1999, never to return to her cluttered little sanctuary from the world.

Casey Jackson was born in 1981 in Baltimore, the first child of John, a marketing manager for an advertising agency, and Karen, a sociologist. A brother, Bobby, followed in 1984 and in 1991 the family moved to Montgomery County, Maryland following John's promotion to advertising executive. Leaving Baltimore behind, they entered a more affluent, suburban lifestyle among the tree-lined avenues of Wheaton's upmarket Connecticut Avenue Estates.

Casey was a high achiever. She was pretty and had a sweetness to her that made her popular but her popularity was never at anybody else's expense. Her peers and her teachers liked her, and words like 'caring', 'thoughtful' and 'bright' were all used in her obituary and at the eulogies at her funeral. She was on the lacrosse team and got straight As in her classes but struggled with low self-esteem. Despite being pretty, popular and smart, she often suffered emotionally if she felt she had let somebody down or hadn't gone the extra mile. Friends described her as always too eager to please, revealing a desperate need for approval.

And nobody's approval was more important to her in the final months of her life than that of Philip Cox.

Casey met Phil in her first year at Wakefield High School though they hardly hit it off immediately. Phil was a boisterous joker while Casey could be painfully shy and, by all accounts, the two never had much to do with each other until their final year. It was their mutual friend Riley Parker who drew the two of them together.

Despite enjoying middle school and adapting well to the move from Baltimore, Casey had struggled with the change of atmosphere and pace that high school brought. She had fallen out with her best friend, Chloe Evans, who had been her companion since fifth grade and Casey entered high school without a strong friendship with anybody. Due to her shyness as much as the clique nature of high school, she struggled to recover her social footing. Riley Parker had been something of a savior for Casey. The two of them bonded over English homework and IT, often hanging out in the school's computer labs.

Riley was part of Phil's clique and had known his best friend Freddie Bronson since kindergarten. Through Riley, Casey was inducted into their world of niche pop culture, Usenet newsgroups, *X-Files* fan fiction and creepy websites of the unexplained. Horror movies and video games weren't Casey's usual interests, but she adapted and learned to talk the talk. For a few months at least, she was finally happy. She had found her clique.

It all seems like an unfair joke when one considers the fact that shortly after Casey had started dating Phil, Phil and Riley began sleeping together.

It is debatable whether Casey knew Phil was cheating on her with her best friend, but examination of Casey's secret diary confirms that she certainly had her suspicions. But there was so much going on in Casey's fragmenting mind in those final months of her life that her suspicions of her boyfriend's infidelity seem almost like a small matter of concern.

However much blame can be placed at Phil and Riley's doors, it is clear that by the spring of 1999, Casey's life had taken a dark turn. She spent more and more time online, delving into the seedier sides of the internet. She chatted to strangers, researched morbid topics and became increasingly paranoid to the point of delusional. The psychological effect of her online activity is clear to see in her erratic behavior in the days before her death. Her diary suggests that she was convinced a shadowy person was stalking her and appearing in the corners of her room at night. She interpreted computer bugs as evidence of somebody watching her.

Her parents noticed nothing strange about her behavior but that is hardly surprising given the extraordinary energy Casey spent on appearing ordinary. She dreaded people finding out what was going on in her mind, fearing the 'crazy' label. *"inside I feel like I'm going to explode!"* she confides to her diary after a particularly trying day.

She did however, reveal her fears to Riley just days before her death. "I didn't listen to her," Riley told police officers. "Nobody did. She died knowing that we didn't believe her."

Casey had no history of psychological problems but then, neither had any of the others which makes what happened to this group of kids in Montgomery County in 1999 so perplexing. Much of their online activity is recorded but competing theories constantly poke at what we can't see for answers. What pieces of the puzzle are missing? Was it all part of an elaborate suicide pact? Was one member of the group not who they seemed? Was it mass hysteria? Then there is the question of outside interference. Online figures pop in and out of the story of Casey Jackson and her friends like walk-on parts in a play and, due to the nature of the internet, are impossible to trace with any certainty. It is undoubtable that what we don't know far outweighs what we do.

No matter how much research we do, no matter how many theories we chew over in our minds, the enigma of Casey Jackson and her friends is bigger than us. Perhaps, instead of looking for the truth of 'what really happened' in Montgomery County in the summer of 1999, we should instead seek simpler answers. There are lessons those teenagers can teach us and we would be foolish to ignore them.

The lesson Casey Jackson teaches us? *Pay attention. Look closer.*

ICQ Conversations between Philip Cox and Riley Parker (05/21/99 – 05/26/99)

Started on Fri May 21 22:06:15 1999

Participants:

Philip Cox – Phil/C

Riley Parker - PrincessKirigoe

Phil/C – Hey. You there?

PrincessKirigoe – Yeah, I'm here. Hi.

Phil/C – You ok?

PrincessKirigoe – I'm coping. Dinner with my parents was super awkward. I think they wanted to comfort me but they just kept asking questions. Ugh.

Phil/C – My mom's the same. I just shut my bedroom door and blast 'Break Stuff' really loud. That always keeps her out.

PrincessKirigoe – I just feel real bad about what we've been doing. Going behind Casey's back you know? I can't help but think that it contributed to her state of mind …

Phil/C – Hey, stop doing that. It was nothing to do with us. Casey had some problems. Real psychological problems. You said yourself that she was seeing stuff …

PrincessKirigoe – Yeah, I know. I just wish we had been there for her more. Both of us.

Phil/C – Yeah. I know. Me too.

PrincessKirigoe – Well, good night. I need to get some sleep. If I can.

Phil/C – Talk to you tomorrow.

PrincessKirigoe – Bye *hugz*

Started on Sat May 22 13:22:52 1999

Participants:

Philip Cox – Phil/C

Riley Parker - PrincessKirigoe

PrincessKirigoe – Hey.

Phil/C – hey

PrincessKirigoe – I know this is really not the time to be thinking about stupid online games, but something really weird happened to me a few moments ago.

Phil/C – What?

PrincessKirigoe – I got a phone call. On the landline. My parents are out and I wasn't online so I picked it up but I can't escape the feeling that it was meant for me. Nobody was on the other end of the line, just a voice recording.

Phil/C – Of what?

PrincessKirigoe – Numbers and letters. Just random shit but read in a child's voice. It was a little girl, I think. I tried to talk to her, but I'm pretty sure it was just a recording. I wrote down some of them, but I missed the first few. I don't know what it was.

Phil/C – You figure it's part of the game?

PrincessKirigoe – I think so. I've heard of players in these games being contacted privately by phone, email, even through snail mail. I just didn't think it would happen to me. I guess I'm through to the next round or whatever :-)

Phil/C – But what are we supposed to do with random numbers? You figure it's a code or something?

PrincessKirigoe – I guess so, but I can't figure it out. And like I said, I missed the first few. I'm going to check the newsgroups to see if anybody else received a similar call.

Phil/C – Let me know

PrincessKirigoe – Will do xx

Started on Sun May 23 12:11:23 1999

Participants:

Philip Cox – Phil/C

Riley Parker – PrincessKirigoe

PrincessKirigoe – Hi.

Phil/C – Hi. Sorry I wasn't online last night. Had some stuff to do.

PrincessKirigoe – No biggie.

Phil/C – You find out anything about your weird phone call?

PrincessKirigoe – Yep. Loads of other guys on Usenet also got the call. It's definitely part of the game.

Phil/C – How come I didn't get one?

PrincessKirigoe – Hmm maybe because I'm the one doing all the hard work? ;-D

Phil/C – Hey! I'm the one who recognized that those torture scenes came from a movie. You wouldn't have solved that puzzle without it. You'd all be looking for a snuff film that didn't exist.

PrincessKirigoe – Yes, sweetie, access to your mental library of horror movies is much appreciated. Seriously, though, you should get on Usenet. Then you can join in and I won't have to relay everything to you. I still have some AOL cds I can give you.

Phil/C – I wouldn't get it. I'm just not a computer nerd like you, Riley ;) Anyway, what did you find out?

PrincessKirigoe – Well, you know that guy, Motix21 I've been talking to? He thinks the calls could be from a numbers station or something like that.

Phil/C – A what?

PrincessKirigoe – A shortwave radio station that broadcasts codes to intelligence officers in foreign countries. Spy stuff.

Phil/C – Cool.

PrincessKirigoe – Until the Men in Black come to erase our memories ... haha :-)

Phil/C – But what does the code say? Has anybody cracked it?

PrincessKirigoe – One guy was able to record the whole thing. It's a tough code but it IS definitely a code. And that means we're meant to decode it.

Phil/C – Well, good luck with that. I'm not a numbers kind of guy.

PrincessKirigoe – No shit ;-)

Started on Sun May 23 22:32:02 1999

Participants:

Philip Cox – Phil/C

Riley Parker – PrincessKirigoe

PrincessKirigoe – Hey. You awake? Shit's going down on Usenet. We solved the code!

Phil/C – Awesome! What does it say?

PrincessKirigoe – Motix is good at this codebreaking stuff and he figured it out. It was a hexadecimal number system!

Phil/C – Babe ....

PrincessKirigoe – Right, sorry. Basically, the encrypted message is another URL. It led to a black screen with a login box. It took us a while, but we were able to hack it. I won't bore you with the details, but it was a pretty easy job. I'm guessing it was another test because you won't believe the message we got onscreen once we were in. Wait, I'll paste it ...

PrincessKirigoe – Greetings and congratulations. You have passed the series of tests I have set you, proving that you are a highly intelligent human being and exactly the sort of person I am looking for to help me with a dangerous but vital task that will open the boundaries of our small world and grant us a true glimpse of the cosmos.

I am Crawdaddy2281. My real name must remain obscure for my safety. I once worked for the JPL (Jet Propulsion Lab) and was part of the Galileo Program, monitoring the probe's progress. About two years ago, we received a high-frequency transmission from the Galileo spacecraft which seemed to have been caused by electromagnetic discharge from Jupiter's electromagnetic field. The signal utterly drowned out the data from the Galileo probe and seemed to be encoded.

I wasn't part of the team assigned to decoding the data but pretty soon, the FBI locked down the lab and controlled access to the signal, spinning cover stories and not letting anybody near the data. It was wild and I knew that something was up. Think about it; a coded signal from outer space that the Feds don't want anybody to know about?

I despise government coverups. If there is contact with alien intelligence, then I believe that every person on this planet has a right to know about it. The feds knew I was a loose cannon because I had started asking too many awkward questions. Pretty soon I got the boot from the JPL on no decent grounds whatsoever. They wanted me out because they knew I could blow the whole thing wide open.

I need to be careful. The feds are watching me, hence all the cloak and dagger stuff online. I know I have found some fellow inquisitive souls who have the skills to help me in my task. Our mission? Hack the server at JPL and extract the data which will prove that we have made contact with extraterrestrial beings. Are you with me? Stand by for further mission instructions.

PrincessKirigoe – Crazy, huh?

Phil/C – So this Crawdaddy2281 is the one who's been steering the whole game? What's the Galileo program?

PrincessKirigoe – A satellite that was launched by the JPL and is currently orbiting Jupiter. He's talking about alien contact, Phil! I don't think it's a game anymore …

Phil/C – It could all be bullshit.

PrincessKirigoe – I know. But what if it isn't? We might actually be breaking a government coverup about extraterrestrial life!

Phil/C – Look, I'm gonna hit the sack, hacker girl. It's too late for this shit and I got training tomorrow.

PrincessKirigoe – Aw, you tired, baby?

Phil/C – I didn't get much sleep last night. Too much shit on my mind.

PrincessKirigoe – I know. I miss her too. Please don't think I'm forgetting her. I just need something to focus on or I'll go insane. Sleep well.

Started on Mon May 24 15:22:09 1999

Participants:

Philip Cox – Phil/C

Riley Parker – PrincessKirigoe

PrincessKirigoe – Hey.

Phil/C – Hey. Jesus Fucking Christ I'm still so pissed!

PrincessKirigoe – I know, right? It was sooooo weird today! I can't believe Freddie would do something like that! Have you heard from him?

Phil/C – Zip. But if I see him again, I'm gonna kick his ass and there won't be any teachers to stop me this time!

PrincessKirigoe – But what the hell was he thinking writing that on Casey's memorial wall anyway? It just doesn't seem like him ...

Phil/C – I keep telling you, Riley, I think he did it.

PrincessKirigoe – Come on. Killed Casey? I just don't see it. Why would he do it?

Phil/C – why would he run through the school hallway butt naked the other week? Because he's fucking unstable. Always has been. Something just pushed him over the edge. It's clear he hated Casey. Probably because he knew she'd never do it with him. That's why he defaced her memorial. And that's why he killed her.

PrincessKirigoe – I don't know. I just feel like there's more to it. I'll call him later and see if I can get through to him.

Phil/C – Don't hold your breath.

PrincessKirigoe – Anyway, you want an update on the whole game that isn't a game?

Phil/C – Sure.

PrincessKirigoe – Well, I've been working with Motix and Crawdaddy on a DoS attack code we can unleash on the JPL network. That should keep their systems busy while we initiate a dictionary attack and try to gain access to their server.

Phil/C – Once again, in English, Riley.

PrincessKirigoe – Sorry. Basically, we're going to overcrowd their system with requests as a distraction. That should give us a small window to crack their password. We'll be ready to download as much data from their servers as we can.

Phil/C – Then what? Go to the media?

PrincessKirigoe – I guess but that's really Crawdaddy's call. He basically wants to blow the lid of the whole thing and I'm going to help him! It's so fucking exciting. But I have a lot of stuff to do. I need to free up space on my hard drive so we can store whatever we find. Crawdaddy said it could be upwards of 5 g.

Phil/C – I'll pretend I know that's a lot.

PrincessKirigoe – Hehe! :-) It is. Speak to you later. Motix is asking me something.

Started on Tue May 25 15:25:02 1999

Participants:

Philip Cox – Phil/C

Riley Parker – PrincessKirigoe

Phil/C – Yo, hacker nerd! How's the great heist going?

PrincessKirigoe – Hehe! We're almost ready. The code we've built is a thing of beauty. JPL won't know what hit them.

Phil/C – I'm still not convinced this isn't just some big hoax. How do you know you'll actually be hacking the JPL?

PrincessKirigoe – If you understood this shit the way I do, you'd know it was the real deal. Crawdaddy is genuine. It's all real!

Started on Tue May 26 20:22:25 1999

Participants:

Philip Cox – Phil/C

Riley Parker – PrincessKirigoe

PrincessKirigoe – Shit, somebody just dropped docs on Crawdaddy!

Phil/C – English, Riley. Do you speak it?

PrincessKirigoe – Somebody outed him on Usenet! His real name and shit! And that's not all. Motix says that there are rumors he's already been arrested!

Phil/C – For what?

PrincessKirigoe – Nobody knows. Something to do with hacking the JPL I guess?

Phil/C – I guess he wasn't as invisible as he thought he was.

PrincessKirigoe – No shit. I'm backing off and so is Motix. We're currently wiping our hard drives. Shit! This is sooooo bad!

Phil/C – Relax, babe. You haven't committed any crime. Nobody knows you were involved.

PrincessKirigoe – You don't understand. If Crawdaddy did something then we could be labeled as accessories! And Crawdaddy knows who we are! Where we live! He called us on our landlines, remember? If he hands us over in exchange for a deal, we're fucked!

Phil/C – Can you hear sirens near your place?

PrincessKirigoe – No. Why?

Phil/C – Two cop cars just shot by here, lights on.

PrincessKirigoe – Are you fucking with me? I swear to God, Phil …

Phil/C – I swear I'm not fucking with you. But chill. It seems like they were heading downtown. I don't think they're coming for you.

PrincessKirigoe – That's a relief.

Phil/C – Two more! There's something going on over on Georgia Avenue.

PrincessKirigoe – Wonder what's up.

News Article from the Montgomery County Sentinel (05/27/99)

TENSE HOSTAGE SITUATION LEAVES TEENAGE BOY DEAD

A student from Wakefield High School was shot dead by police yesterday evening after what has been described as an attempt to abduct an infant.

Geraldine Eastwood, a twenty-seven-year-old mother of two, was buying groceries at the Wheaton Shopping Center at around 7:25 last night when her youngest son, eight-month-old James, was taken from his stroller by the suspect. Miss. Eastwood had her back to the stroller at the time while she tried to stop her five-year-old from running off and did not see the suspect pick James up.

The suspect, identified as Frederick Bronson, nineteen-years-old, fled the scene with the baby amid cries of protest from passersby who alerted Miss. Eastwood to the abduction of her child. Some tried to stop the suspect, but he revealed that he was armed with a kitchen knife and took refuge in a laundromat on Georgia Avenue.

Montgomery County Department of Police 4th District officers were dispatched to the laundromat where the suspect was holding several customers hostage in addition to baby James. The suspect appeared to be in a distressed state and seemed apologetic for his actions.

Witnesses said that he kept repeating; "She made me do it!"

The suspect did not comply with commands from officers to hand the baby over or to drop the knife, resulting in an officer shooting the suspect. Officers rendered aid to him, however he was pronounced dead at the scene. Baby James was returned unharmed to his mother.

Rumors that the suspect was friends with Casey Jackson, another student of Wakefield High, whose body was found last Thursday evening, have not yet been confirmed.

PROFILE OF FREDERICK BRONSON

From *Ghost in the Machine: The Montgomery County Murders* by David Williamson (Tulane University Press: 2001), p. 57:

Freddie Bronson was the class clown. There are no two ways about it. On the last day of his freshman year at Wakefield High, he brought an inflatable sex doll into school and set her up in the office chair of the school librarian Mrs. Penshaw, a strict, no-nonsense woman with deep-set Christian values.

Freddie managed to evade the ensuing furor with the luck and dexterity of a cat. Officially, the identity of the perpetrator went unknown. Unofficially, everybody knew it was Freddie. It was a pattern that defined most of his life. He loved pranks and had a seemingly innate ability to wangle himself out of trouble. The closest scrape he had was at the age of thirteen when he purchased a pack of condoms on a school trip and turned them into water balloons (a certain theme is detected in the nature of Freddie's pranks). Freddie was suspended for the incident and would have been expelled had it not been for the smooth talking of his father, and all agreed that, once again, he had got off lucky.

In the spring of 1999, however, Freddie's luck ran out.

A native of Wheaton, Freddie was born in 1981 to Mark Bronson, an attorney and Christina Plaza, a homemaker. The Bronsons lived at the same affluent Connecticut Avenue Estates address all Freddie's life, only two streets away from the residence of Casey Jackson. He had a sister, two years younger than him, who adored him despite his penchant for pressing peoples' buttons. "He was all heart," Violet Bronson says. "Some people just didn't get his humor but none of it was malicious. He just wanted to have a good time. If he could make people laugh, then great but it was mainly to amuse himself and I think people get the wrong impression about him because of that."

Freddie was a nervous talker, his speech pattern reaching the speed of a drum machine when he became excited. He would gush about whatever he was passionate about and he was passionate about a lot of things. Horror movies interested him in particular, a hobby he shared with his best friend Philip Cox. At sixteen, they snuck in to see *Scream*, the horror blockbuster of 1996 which had a profound effect on them. "They were obsessed by that movie," said friend Dwight Ulrich. "Freddie had the mask and everything and would use it to prank people, scare them, you know?"

While Freddie was a joker with a wicked tongue, he was generally considered a nice enough kid but when he was with Phil, a change in personality was noticeable. He would often get swept up in Phil's bullying ways, joining in and always looking to Phil for approval. It was clear to all who the dominant personality was in the friendship. Phil was bigger, more intimidating and had a nasty streak which, combined with Freddie's penchant for practical jokes, made them a terrorizing duo for many in the grades below them.

But unlike Phil, Freddie was entirely uninterested in sports. He was far more bookish than his best friend and was a voracious reader of science fiction and horror, citing H. P. Lovecraft and Stephen King as favorites. Computers also elicited a fascination in him, and he had been a member of various computer clubs since the seventh grade. He could often be found in the school's computer lab with his friend Riley Parker whom he had known since kindergarten. Riley shared his interest in computers and the internet and they both created their own websites and contributed to Usenet newsgroups.

It was perhaps Freddie's desire to delve deeper than his peers and his fascination with the unexplained and the unexplored which led to his calamity. Like Casey Jackson, Freddie became obsessed with the darker corners of the internet and the effect it had on him is comparable. Both displayed symptoms of paranoia and delusion before their deaths.

Casey's death hit him hard according to his sister. His final days were marred by depression and erratic behavior, but she insists that this started before Casey's demise. "He was a completely different person in his last month," she says. "Like there was some new influence in his life that he didn't want to tell anybody about."

On 18 May, Freddie ran naked through his school hallways, a prank considered excessive even by his standards. The ensuing outrage and talks of suspension were sidelined by the death of Casey two days later. If Freddie was devastated by the death of his friend, he did a good job of concealing it, writing a hate-filled message about her on the memorial board put up in her name the Monday after her death.

The vitriolic message calling her a 'slut' and that she now "rots in Hell" is the strongest argument for those who are convinced that Freddie murdered Casey or at least hounded her to her death. Was Freddie secretly in love with Casey and resentful that she had chosen his best friend over him? There is little evidence to suggest that he had any interest in her other than as a 'hot chick' (a designation he honored many of Wakefield High's female students with). According to classmates, Freddie was a horny joker but not a lovestruck one. "It was all about sex," fellow student Sarah Wills says dismissively. "He was only interested in women's bodies, and I don't think he was capable of loving them or seeing them as anything other than objects". Despite his constant boasting to the contrary, Freddie most likely died a virgin.

Even before evidence was found to support the fact, Violet Bronson was convinced that somebody had put her brother up to the tasteless stunts in the last week of his life. "He was being threatened," she says. "Goaded into doing things like a sick game of Truth or Dare. My brother was like a kid under somebody's thumb in his last days. He was miserable and frightened. He didn't hate Casey and he certainly didn't kill her."

But who was threatening Freddie? Before he was gunned down by police in a laundromat during a bizarre attempt to abduct a baby, he cried out several times that "She made me do it!" Who did? Inspection of Freddie's computer after his death reveal emails from a certain 'Melissa Smith' who, it will be revealed, played the biggest role in Freddie's death.

Emails between Frederick Bronson and 'Melissa Smith' (04/26/99 – 05/26/99)

Date: 04/26/1999

Time: 13:42

From: Melissa Smith <mmmwonderland@[omitted].com>

To: Frederick Bronson <freddiesfingers@[omitted].com>

Subject: Hello

Hi!!!!!

I'm so glad you decided to give me your email address last night. Forums are fun and all, but email is so much more intimate. It suggests a level of trust, don't you think? So, now we're past the whole A/S/L bit, how about you tell me more about yourself? I'll go first hehe :)

I like red wine, dance music, romantic movies (with a lot of SEX in them) and having a good time. I'm tall, brunette and have a great figure if I do say so myself ;) In private I tend to lean towards the darker side of things... Think you can handle me?

Your turn...

Hugz

Melissa

Date: 04/26/1999

Time: 15:56

From: Melissa Smith <mmmwonder-land@[omitted].com>

To: Frederick Bronson <freddiesfingers@[omitted].com>

Subject: Hello

Hello???????

Date: 04/26/1999

Time: 16:22

From: Frederick Bronson <freddiesfin-gers@[omitted].com>

To: Melissa Smith <mmmwonderland@[omitted].com>

Subject: Re: Hello

Hi Melissa,

Sorry, I only just read your email. I just got home from work. Busy day. Yeah, it's great to speak to you more privately. And thank you for the extra info about yourself. I'm having fun picturing you. I like brunettes ;o)

As for me, I guess you could say I'm tall, dark and handsome (not to boast or anything - haha). I work in advertising and I like industrial bands like Rammstein and NIN. Oh, and I LOVE horror movies. Seriously, ask me anything about horror and I bet you can't catch me out.

Not much for red wine personally, but I do like beer and a good whiskey.

By the way, are you a goth? Nothing personal, I just wondered at the 'darker side' comment...

Freddie

Date: 04/26/1999

Time: 16:46

From: Melissa Smith mmmwonderland@[omitted].com

To: Frederick Bronson <freddiesfingers@[omitted].com>

Subject: Re: Hello

Haha no, I'm not a goth :) I just meant I'm into the kinkier side of human nature. It's a little dark for some people who can't handle it.

Horror movies, huh? I like them too. Especially the gory ones. Which one's your favorite?

Hugz

Melissa

P.S. I hope you don't do this with a lot of girls you meet online. Send them private emails, I mean. I'd like to be the only one. I just want to know where I stand :)

Date: 04/26/1999

Time: 16:46

From: Melissa Smith mmmwonderland@[omitted].com

To: Frederick Bronson <freddiesfingers@[omitted].com>

Subject: Re: Hello

203⊥⊥Ö1l1œ¥96 53701 85○8 ±21512⫠‖ e81 `Ù1 ♂ët l3õ◘

Date: 04/26/1999

Time: 16:47

From: Frederick Bronson <freddiesfin-
gers@[omitted].com>

To: Melissa Smith mmmwonderland@[omitted].com

Subject: Re: Hello

Haha! What?!

Date: 04/26/1999

Time: 16:47

From: Melissa Smith mmmwonderland@[omitted].com

To: Frederick Bronson <freddiesfingers@[omitted].com>

Subject: Re: Hello

Sorry. That was weird. Don't know what happened there.

Date: 04/26/1999

Time: 21:31

From: Frederick Bronson <freddiesfin-gers@[omitted].com>

To: Melissa Smith mmmwonderland@[omitted].com

Subject: Re: Hello

Hey,

It wouldn't have bothered me if you were a goth. We have a few of them at my school. They're OK but everybody gives them a wide berth because they're so obsessed with death and stuff. Actually, I find them kind of sexy in a morbid way. Are you sure you're not a little bit goth (wink wink)? And what sort of kinky are we talking about here...?

My favorite horror movie is probably Scream. Or maybe Candyman. You?

Freddie

P.S. No, I don't usually do this with girls I meet online. In fact, you're the first that I've given my email address to. Speaking of which, at what point should we share pictures? I'm dying to know what you look like :oD

Date: 04/26/1999

Time: 21:35

From: Melissa Smith mmmwonderland@[omitted].com

To: Frederick Bronson <freddiesfingers@[omitted].com>

Subject: Re: Hello

School? I thought you said you had a job in advertising…
Just how old are you, mister?

Date: 04/26/1999

Time: 21:47

From: Frederick Bronson <freddiesfin-
gers@[omitted].com>

To: Melissa Smith mmmwonderland@[omitted].com

Subject: Re: Hello

Shit. I messed up here and I'm really sorry. You found
me out. I'm still in high school but I'm graduating this
summer! I'm nineteen but I'm big for my age and people
say I'm pretty mature. Look, I'm really sorry if I screwed
all this up and you don't want to talk to me anymore.

I understand if you're pissed. But I hope you're not.

Hugz

Freddie

Date: 04/26/1999

Time: 22:12

From: Melissa Smith mmmwonderland@[omitted].com

To: Frederick Bronson <freddiesfingers@[omitted].com>

Subject: Re: Hello

Naughty, naughty! Bad boy telling lies ...

I'm kidding. It's fine. I figured you might be a little younger than you claimed. Just something about the way you speak. You don't sound like a boring adult who works in advertising.

I have a confession to make. I'm a little younger than I said I was too. Would you hate me if I said I was only eighteen? I guess we're both naughty little liars who deserve to be punished. But between you and me, I'd rather be on the receiving end if you know what I mean ;)

Oh, I've been meaning to ask; what does your email address mean? Freddies Fingers? Hmmm... It makes me think about your fingers and how thick they might be.

I want your fingers inside me.

thinking dirty thoughts

Melissa

Date: 04/27/1999

Time: 16:11

From: Frederick Bronson <freddiesfin-gers@[omitted].com>

To: Melissa Smith mmmwonderland@[omitted].com

Subject: Ummmmmmmm……

Um. Wow. That was quite the come on last night. Don't get me wrong, I like it. I like it a lot. Sorry I didn't reply immediately. I was kind of lost for words and it was getting late. I guess I needed to sleep on it before I gave you a response.

With regard to your question … yeah, Freddies Fingers refers to my digits and the use they might be put to. Not everyone gets it but some smart cookies (like you) do.

Sooo… you never answered my question. You said you were kinky. How kinky and what sort of kinky?

Waiting in heated anticipation,

Freddie('s Fingers)

Date: 04/27/1999

Time: 16:12

From: Melissa Smith mmmwonderland@[omitted].com

To: Frederick Bronson <freddiesfingers@[omitted].com>

Subject: Re: Ummmmmmmm……

Hey there, Stud.

When I say kinky, I mean whips and chains BDSM stuff. You down?

If you are, then let's make a date. Email is too slow for a real scene. I want instant responses! Want to take this over to ICQ for a while?

Please say yes.

Mel

Date: 04/27/1999

Time: 16:24

From: Frederick Bronson <freddiesfin-gers@[omitted].com>

To: Melissa Smith mmmwonderland@[omitted].com

Subject: Re: Ummmmmmmm......

OK. You're on. How about we hook up later at around seven? Got a few things to do first so I can give you all my attention ;)

By the way, I haven't done this before so apologies beforehand.

Freddie

Date: 04/27/1999

Time: 16:29

From: Melissa Smith mmmwonderland@[omitted].com

To: Frederick Bronson <freddiesfingers@[omitted].com>

Subject: Re: Ummmmmmmm......

First time for me too :) Don't worry, I'm sure you'll be fine. Just know that I like being told what to do and being punished when I'm bad ;)

Seven it is then. I'll be waiting. IF I can hold out that long …

I'm so wet just thinking about the things you'll do to me.

xoxo

Mel

Date: 04/28/1999

Time: 16:11

From: Frederick Bronson <freddiesfin-gers@[omitted].com>

To: Melissa Smith mmmwonderland@[omitted].com

Subject: Thinking about you …

Hey,

Last night was awesome. I kept thinking about it all thru today. You were hot!!! Are you sure you haven't done this before? I felt like I was dealing with a pro :)

xoxo

Freddie

Date: 04/28/1999

Time: 16:21

From: Melissa Smith mmmwonderland@[omitted].com

To: Frederick Bronson <freddiesfingers@[omitted].com>

Subject: Re: Ummmmmmmm......

Oh, Freddie, it was good for me too! I can't tell you how long I've been waiting for somebody to fulfil me like you did last night. I had a feeling you'd be a wonderful Dom. I could just tell ...

My body is so bruised and welted that I can barely sit or lie down but it feels good because I know that the pain is from you.

Your very obedient and chastised Sub,

Mel

xxxxxx

Date: 04/28/1999

Time: 16:22

From: Frederick Bronson <freddiesfin-gers@[omitted].com>

To: Melissa Smith mmmwonderland@[omitted].com

Subject: Re: Ummmmmmmm......

Uhhh, how do you mean your body is bruised and welted? From cybersex?!?

Date: 04/28/1999

Time: 16:26

From: Melissa Smith mmmwonderland@[omitted].com

To: Frederick Bronson <freddiesfingers@[omitted].com>

Subject: Re: Ummmmmmmm......

I used a wire coat hanger to whip myself every time you said that you were punishing me, stroke for stroke. That way your words physically hurt me. You reached out through the internet and sternly disciplined me, and it felt so real. It WAS real! I can still feel the sting of your touch...

I can't wait to be punished by you again. But I need some time to recover. I'm black and blue and I know that I'll be a good girl for a while. But just you wait. I know I'll be bad again and then ... it's coat hanger time ;)

xxxxxxxx

Mel

Date: 04/28/1999

Time: 16:37

From: Frederick Bronson <freddiesfin-gers@[omitted].com>

To: Melissa Smith mmmwonderland@[omitted].com

Subject: Re: Ummmmmmmmm……

Jesus, Melissa.

I didn't know that you'd do that to yourself. I thought it was just fantasy. Are you sure you're OK? I mean, a wire coat hanger? If I'd have known, then I might have gone a bit easier on you.

Freddie

Date: 04/28/1999

Time: 16:51

From:

To: Melissa Smith mmmwonderland@[omitted].com
Frederick Bronson <freddiesfingers@[omitted].com>

Subject: Re: Ummmmmmmm……

Don't say that. Don't ruin it.

I need you Freddie. I need your tough love because it's the only way I can feel good about myself.

I want us to do it again, and soon. But not just yet. In the meantime, I hope you'll be thinking of me as I'm thinking of you. What is it they say about absence or abstinence or something and the heart growing fonder?

Until next time, my master ;)

xoxo

Mel

Date: 05/03/1999

Time: 21:22

From: Melissa Smith mmmwonderland@[omitted].com

To: Frederick Bronson <freddiesfingers@[omitted].com>

Subject: It's our one week anniversary...

Hey there, Stud. You're not online so I'm sending you this little reminder. I hope you read it soon.

Do you remember what we were doing around this time one week ago? I do. You had me hogtied over a glass table and were whipping me severely. The bruises have only just gone away and my pussy gets wet whenever I think of you. It's ready for you again. I want you in me. My body is ready for your punishment.

ICQ?

Kiss-kiss

Mel

Date: 05/03/1999

Time: 21:35

From: Frederick Bronson <freddiesfin-gers@[omitted].com>

To: Melissa Smith mmmwonderland@[omitted].com

Subject: Re: It's our one week anniversary...

Hi Mel.

Sure, I can ICQ. I'm ready for you too.

No wire coat hangers, this time, huh? Let's keep it strictly verbal.

Freddie

Date: 05/03/1999

Time: 23:53

From: Frederick Bronson <freddiesfin-gers@[omitted].com>

To: Melissa Smith mmmwonderland@[omitted].com

Subject: Re: It's our one week anniversary...

Mel, I'm going to bed now and I just wanted to check that you're OK. That was seriously fucked up and I have to be honest, I'm not really into that level of brutality. I mean, I'm kinky and all, I guess you know that by now, but meat hooks and barbed wire? What you're doing to yourself is wrong. Unhealthy.

You might need help.

Freddie

Date: 05/04/1999

Time: 00:01

From: Melissa Smith mmmwonderland@[omitted].com

To: Frederick Bronson <freddiesfingers@[omitted].com>

Subject: Re: It's our one week anniversary…

I'm sorry if I scared you off. My passions can get a little hot and heavy for some people. I thought you were up for this? The cuts in my flesh will heal. They always do.

You can't leave me like this. I will really hurt myself if you break this off now. I have a bottle of bleach and an enema on standby if I get too depressed …

xoxo

Mel

Date: 05/04/1999

Time: 16:25

From: Frederick Bronson <freddiesfin-gers@[omitted].com>

To: Melissa Smith mmmwonderland@[omitted].com

Subject: Please don't

Melissa,

Please don't hurt yourself any more on my account. I know this might all be bullshit and that you may have no intention of hurting yourself and that you never whipped yourself with a coat hanger, but in the event that you really are that messed up, I'm begging you, not to hurt yourself anymore. I'm not worth it.

Freddie

Date: 05/04/1999

Time: 16:27

From: Melissa Smith mmmwonderland@[omitted].com

To: Frederick Bronson <freddiesfingers@[omitted].com>

Subject: Re: Please don't

Is there somebody else?

Date: 05/04/1999

Time: 16:27

From: Melissa Smith mmmwonderland@[omitted].com

To: Frederick Bronson <freddiesfingers@[omitted].com>

Subject: Re: Please don't

No, there's nobody else. I just think we should cool it for
a while. Maybe some perspective will help you
understand that this isn't healthy.

Date: 05/04/1999

Time: 16:27

From: Melissa Smith mmmwonderland@[omitted].com

To: Frederick Bronson <freddiesfingers@[omitted].com>

Subject: Re: Please don't

Liar! I fffffff8 ±21512-‖ ound her!found her! You thought you could sneak around behiiiii ¶¶≈∑ nd my back and have cybersex with some fucking whore?!?

I

Date: 05/04/1999

Time: 16:45

From: Frederick Bronson <freddiesfin-gers@[omitted].com>

To: Melissa Smith mmmwonderland@[omitted].com

Subject: Re: Please don't

Melissa,

I think we should stop contacting each other for a while. This is seriously beginning to freak me out.

Please don't do anything dumb.

Freddie

Date: 05/11/1999

Time: 13:11

From: Melissa Smith mmmwonderland@[omitted].com

To: Frederick Bronson <freddiesfingers@[omitted].com>

Subject: foundherfoundherfoundher!!!!!!!!!

Freddie ....

Have you heard anything from your little bitch Amy?

xxx

Mel

Date: 05/11/1999

Time: 16:09

From: Frederick Bronson <freddiesfin-gers@[omitted].com>

To: Melissa Smith mmmwonderland@[omitted].com

Subject: Re: Please don't

She's stopped talking to me. How did you find out about her and what did you tell her?

Date: 05/11/1999

Time: 16:10

From: Melissa Smith mmmwonderland@[omitted].com

To: Frederick Bronson <freddiesfingers@[omitted].com>

Subject: Re: foundherfoundherfoundher!!!!!!!!!

Date: 05/08/1999

Time: 23:53

From: Frederick Bronson <freddiesfin-gers@[omitted].com>

To: AmyGeorge@[omitted].com

Subject: Hello

Hi Amy.

Thanks for giving me your email address. Email is so much more intimate than instant messaging, don't you think?

Do you know what would be even more intimate? If we met up and had some fun. I'm into the darker, kinkier side of sex and I hope you're the same. I like BDSM, whips and chains etc. You up for it?

Right now I'm fantasizing about fucking you in the ass with a spiked dildo while I whip your tits bloody. I want to tie you up and hurt you in ways you can't imagine.

Here's a screenshot of my web history to get an idea of the things I'd like to do to you ...

Image withheld by the Montgomery County Police Department

Your future fuckbuddy,

Freddie's fat juicy Fingers

Date: 05/11/1999

Time: 16:16

From: Frederick Bronson <freddiesfin-gers@[omitted].com>

To: Melissa Smith mmmwonderland@[omitted].com

Subject: Re: foundherfoundherfoundher!!!!!!!!!

How the fuck did you send an email from my account? And how do you have access to my web history?

Date: 05/11/1999

Time: 16:17

From: Melissa Smith mmmwonderland@[omitted].com

To: Frederick Bronson <freddiesfingers@[omitted].com>

Subject: Re: foundherfoundherfoundher!!!!!!!!!

I'm a dab hand at hacking so consider yourself HACKED!

Now, what will you do to stop me from sending the same stuff to your friends in real life? How about Riley Parker or Casey Jackson? What will THEY think of your exotic tastes, huh?

Date: 05/11/1999

Time: 16:17

From: Frederick Bronson <freddiesfin-
gers@[omitted].com>

To: Melissa Smith mmmwonderland@[omitted].com

Subject: Re: foundherfoundherfoundher!!!!!!!!!

What do you want from me?

Date: 05/11/1999

Time: 16:19

From: Melissa Smith mmmwonderland@[omitted].com

To: Frederick Bronson <freddiesfingers@[omitted].com>

Subject: Re: foundherfoundherfoundher!!!!!!!!!

Another ICQ session and this time show some willing. I
want you to go REAL hard on me. Make me suffer. Use
all your anger at me for what I've done and make me
bleed.

Hugz

Mel

Date: 05/11/1999

Time: 17:35

From: Frederick Bronson <freddiesfin-
gers@[omitted].com>

To: AmyGeorge@[omitted].com

Subject: Please open this. The last email was NOT from
me!!!!

Hi Amy

I can only apologize for the sick and deranged email you
received from my account a few days ago. Somebody
hacked my account and that email was NOT from me!

I am dealing with a psycho crazy person online and she
somehow got into my email. I'm going to be getting the
police involved so you needn't worry about any more
disgusting messages from me.

Oh, and she also somehow falsified my web history. I
didn't visit those sites.

Sorry again.

Freddie

Date: 05/11/1999

Time: 20:07

From: Melissa Smith mmmwonderland@[omitted].com

To: Frederick Bronson <freddiesfingers@[omitted].com>

Subject: Re: foundherfoundherfoundher!!!!!!!!!!

If you ever tell anyone about me again, your life will be over, you pathetic worm of a human being. I control your email, your ICQ account and I can destroy your life if I want to. If you switch to a new account or try to evade me in any way, I will FUCKING ruin you.

And if you get the cops involved, the same rules apply :)

Hugz,

Mel

P.S. Thank you for the scene tonight. It was just what I hoped for. I am so sore and have only just stopped bleeding. Until next time ... xxxx

Date: 05/14/1999

Time: 13:13

From: Melissa Smith mmmwonderland@[omitted].com

To: Frederick Bronson <freddiesfingers@[omitted].com>

Subject: New rules

Hey there, Stud.

I know it hasn't even been a week since our last scene, but I just can't stop thinking about you. And I want to take our games to the next level.

I want you to do something FOR me this time, not to me. Let's consider it a kind of truth or dare game.

Here's your dare.

There's an old lady who lives two doors down from you. Very prim and proper. Neat little rose garden. You know the one. I want you to spray paint a big penis on the side of her house and send a picture to me. You do have a digital camera, right?

Date: 05/14/1999

Time: 16:10

From: Frederick Bronson <freddiesfingers@[omitted].com>

To: Melissa Smith mmmwonderland@[omitted].com

Subject: Re: New rules

How do you know where I live?

Date: 05/14/1999

Time: 16:11

From: Melissa Smith mmmwonderland@[omitted].com

To: Frederick Bronson <freddiesfingers@[omitted].com>

Subject: Re: New rules

That's the least of your concerns. I know everything about you, Frederick Bronson. Do what I ask or face the consequences. Do it tonight.

Hugz,

Mel

Date: 05/15/1999

Time: 00:16

From: Frederick Bronson <freddiesfin-gers@[omitted].com>

To: Melissa Smith mmmwonderland@[omitted].com

Subject: Re: New rules

Image withheld by the Montgomery County Police Department

Date: 05/15/1999

Time: 11:24

From: Melissa Smith mmmwonderland@[omitted].com

To: Frederick Bronson <freddiesfingers@[omitted].com>

Subject: Re: New rules

Very good! I'm impressed, Stud. You have quite the artistic streak.

I'll be in touch regarding your next dare.

xoxo

Mel

Date: 05/17/1999

Time: 13:21

From: Melissa Smith mmmwonderland@[omitted].com

To: Frederick Bronson <freddiesfingers@[omitted].com>

Subject: Re: New rules

Hey there, Stud.

Next dare. Run through your school hallways butt naked. Tomorrow.

xxx Mel

Date: 05/17/1999

Time: 16:08

From: Frederick Bronson <freddiesfin-gers@[omitted].com>

To: Melissa Smith mmmwonderland@[omitted].com

Subject: Re: New rules

Fuck you I'm not doing that.

Date: 05/17/1999

Time: 16:10

From: Melissa Smith mmmwonderland@[omitted].com

To: Frederick Bronson <freddiesfingers@[omitted].com>

Subject: Re: New rules

Hey, you want to know a secret? I lied about my age.

I'm only 14.

Wouldn't the cops be interested in seeing our ICQ sessions? Seeing what you made me do to my body? I had to go to the doctor after our last scene and he said I might need surgery. He also asked a lot of questions about how I got these injuries. I didn't tell. Yet ...

Date: 05/17/1999

Time: 16:12

From: Frederick Bronson <freddiesfin-gers@[omitted].com>

To: Melissa Smith mmmwonderland@[omitted].com

Subject: Re: New rules

Bullshit. I'm starting to think that nothing you have ever said to me is true. You're a sick, fucked up grown ass adult. You've done nothing to yourself and you sure as hell can't trick me into thinking you're 14.

Date: 05/17/1999

Time: 16:22

From: Melissa Smith mmmwonderland@[omitted].com

To: Frederick Bronson <freddiesfingers@[omitted].com>

Subject: Re: New rules

Oh, yes I am.

Here's some proof. Take a look at this picture of me. See what you've done to me?

Image withheld by the Montgomery County Police Department

Date: 05/17/1999

Time: 16:22

From: Frederick Bronson <freddiesfin-gers@[omitted].com>

To: Melissa Smith mmmwonderland@[omitted].com

Subject: Re: New rules

Jesus christ is that real?

Date: 05/17/1999

Time: 16:24

From: Melissa Smith mmmwonderland@[omitted].com

To: Frederick Bronson <freddiesfingers@[omitted].com>

Subject: Re: New rules

Real as a heart attack, baby.

Truth or Dare. You dare to do what I tell you, or I tell everybody the truth about you. That you're a sick, depraved pervert who hooks up with underage girls online and make them mutilate themselves.

Date: 05/17/1999

Time: 16:25

From: Frederick Bronson <freddiesfin-gers@[omitted].com>

To: Melissa Smith mmmwonderland@[omitted].com

Subject: Re: New rules

How will you know that I did it? You want a photo this time too?

Date: 05/17/1999

Time: 16:25

From: Melissa Smith mmmwonderland@[omitted].com

To: Frederick Bronson <freddiesfingers@[omitted].com>

Subject: Re: New rules

No need for a photo. I'll just know.

Date: 05/18/1999

Time: 15:14

From: Melissa Smith mmmwonderland@[omitted].com

To: Frederick Bronson <freddiesfingers@[omitted].com>

Subject: Re: New rules

Good boy. You caused quite a stir hehe :) Hope you didn't get too much detention.

xxxx

Mel

Date: 05/18/1999

Time: 16:10

From: Frederick Bronson <freddiesfin-gers@[omitted].com>

To: Melissa Smith mmmwonderland@[omitted].com

Subject: Re: New rules

Wait, are you somebody at my school?

Date: 05/22/1999

Time: 13:28

From: Melissa Smith mmmwonderland@[omitted].com

To: Frederick Bronson <freddiesfingers@[omitted].com>

Subject: Re: New rules

So sorry to hear about your friend Casey and her untimely death. So sad :(

There is a memorial board to her in your school. On Monday I want you to write the following; "Casey Jackson was a fucking slut and now she rots in hell." Then sign your name. That last bit is important.

Hugz,

Mel

Date: 05/22/1999

Time: 13:41

From: Frederick Bronson <freddiesfin-gers@[omitted].com>

To: Melissa Smith mmmwonderland@[omitted].com

Subject: Re: New rules

Please stop doing this. What are you getting out of this?

Date: 05/22/1999

Time: 13:43

From: Melissa Smith mmmwonderland@[omitted].com

To: Frederick Bronson <freddiesfingers@[omitted].com>

Subject: Re: New rules

Do it or I release everything I've got on you to the cops and your friends and family. Your life will be over.

Date: 05/24/1999

Time: 16:14

From: Frederick Bronson <freddiesfin-gers@[omitted].com>

To: Melissa Smith mmmwonderland@[omitted].com

Subject: Re: New rules

OK, I did it. Everybody hates my guts. Are you happy now?

Date: 05/24/1999

Time: 16:15

From: Melissa Smith mmmwonderland@[omitted].com

To: Frederick Bronson <freddiesfingers@[omitted].com>

Subject: Re: New rules

For the time being :)

Date: 05/26/1999

Time: 13:03

From: Melissa Smith mmmwonderland@[omitted].com

To: Frederick Bronson <freddiesfingers@[omitted].com>

Subject: Re: New rules

Next dare, Stud. And we're upping the stakes.

I want you to kidnap a baby.

Go down to the Wheaton Shopping Center and find a baby. I don't care if it's in a stroller or a vehicle or if you have to wrench it from its mother's arms, but get a baby and hold on to it until you receive further instructions from me.

Date: 05/26/1999

Time: 16:07

From: Frederick Bronson <freddiesfin-gers@[omitted].com>

To: Melissa Smith mmmwonderland@[omitted].com

Subject: Re: New rules

Are you fucking nuts? There's no way I'm kidnapping a baby!!!!

Date: 05/26/1999

Time: 16:08

From: Melissa Smith mmmwonderland@[omitted].com

To: Frederick Bronson <freddiesfingers@[omitted].com>

Subject: Re: New rules

Then I guess the world is going to see Frederick Bronson in a whole new light. Borrowing a baby for a few hours will seem like small potatoes compared to what you've done to an underage girl.

Tick-tock, you have until dark to get this done.

X Mel

This was the last email Frederick Bronson received from 'Melissa Smith'. He was killed later that night in a police standoff while attempting to carry out her instructions. Analysis of Mr. Bronson's computer revealed that the emails from the elusive Miss. Smith originated from the same IP address as the recipient suggesting that Mr. Bronson was sending them to himself. The ICQ chat sessions referred to in the emails have never been recovered.

Beauty in Darkness: The Online Journal of Chloe Evans (05/27/99)

May 27, 1999

I just don't know what the fuck is happening. Yesterday, another kid from my school got killed. He was a close friend of Casey's and the way he got killed is another mystery.

His name was Freddie and at some point last night he grabbed a baby from its stroller down at the shopping center. Everybody freaked out of course and the cops were called while Freddie hid in a laundromat. They eventually gunned him down.

I didn't really mind Freddie all that much. He was kind of a dick but that was largely the company he kept. He didn't deserve to die like that and nobody knows what the fuck he was doing kidnapping a baby. It was totally insane. Everyone's talking about it and saying what a weird creep he was but I know there's something more to this. Freddie was the kind of guy who would do anything for a laugh but nobody laughs at kidnapping. There has to be some other motivation behind it. Also, he wrote some vitriolic shit on Casey's memorial a couple of days ago which had everybody losing their shit. He was her friend so I don't get that either. Something was going on with him and I just know its somehow connected to Casey's death.

My dad is pretty freaked over the whole thing. He's always been a bit overprotective of me but since these deaths, he seems worried that I'll be next. I keep trying to convince him that I'm not a part of whatever the hell is going on. Whatever it is, it involves that group of friends; Casey, Freddie, Phil and Riley. The police are just as confused as everybody else is.

I still don't think it's drugs. Freddie, maybe. But not Casey.

\m/ Stay dark and beautiful, gothlings.

ICQ Conversations between Riley Parker and Philip Cox (05/07/99 – 05/31/99)

Started on Thu May 27 15:06:12 1999

Participants:

Philip Cox – Phil/C

Riley Parker - PrincessKirigoe

PrincessKirigoe – Seriously, what the fuck is going on?

Phil/C – Yeah, I know. First Casey and now Freddie. Getting pretty sick of talking to the cops.

PrincessKirigoe – I'm so fucking ruined by this. Casey and Freddie were my best friends.

Phil/C – I'm sorry, babe. Shall I come over? Maybe it's best if we're not alone.

PrincessKirigoe – Tonight's not a good time. My parents are in full-on sympathy mode. My mom is making food for Freddie's family and we're going over there later. Like they're going to want to eat anything! Why is food the first thing anybody can think of when somebody dies? It just seems so superficial.

Phil/C – I just don't get it. I mean, Freddie was acting pretty weird, but kidnapping a baby? What the hell was he thinking?

PrincessKirigoe – Super weird. Something was going on with him, I'm sure of it.

Phil/C – Still think he didn't murder Casey?

PrincessKirigoe – Yeah. Sure, it looks even worse now, and the cops are beginning to think it's an open and shut case but what's stealing somebody's kid got to do with what happened to Casey?

Phil/C – I'm not convinced either way. If he didn't kill her then their deaths are connected somehow, that much I do know.

PrincessKirigoe – I gotta go. Mom wants help in the kitchen.

Phil/C – Speak to you later?

PrincessKirigoe – Sure. Xx

Started on Thu May 27 21:42:36 1999

Participants:

Philip Cox – Phil/C

Riley Parker - PrincessKirigoe

PrincessKirigoe – Hey. We're back.

Phil/C – How did it go?

PrincessKirigoe –Painful. His parents just kept crying and mine didn't know what to do. The only one who was lucid enough to talk to was Violet. We had a pretty long chat in her room. I think Freddie was being blackmailed.

Phil/C – Huh?

PrincessKirigoe – She said that he was living in fear in the last few days of his life. And his weird behavior feels too much like a bunch of dares. That's what she thinks, anyway. He was just not himself and she thinks somebody had some influence over him.

Phil/C – Dares?

PrincessKirigoe – Yeah. Like, if you don't do this dare then I'll do something really bad to you?

Phil/C – Like what?

PrincessKirigoe – I don't know. Freddy spent a lot of time online. Maybe somebody got to him, found out stuff about him. Threatened to drop docs, that sort of thing. Maybe it was his mysterious girlfriend?

Phil/C – That's what I was just thinking.

PrincessKirigoe – Did anybody ever find out who she was?

Phil/C – I was never too sure she really existed. Freddy had a pretty big mouth.

PrincessKirigoe – Yeah. I miss him.

Phil/C – We need to find out what the hell happened. The cops don't know shit.

PrincessKirigoe – But where do we start?

Phil/C – I don't know

Started on Fri May 28 22:14:32 1999

Participants:

Philip Cox – Phil/C

Riley Parker – PrincessKirigoe

PrincessKirigoe – Hey. Well, today was super awkward.

Phil/C – Yeah. If I have to sit through another gymnasium memorial speech I'm going to slit my fucking wrists.

PrincessKirigoe – Don't say that. Don't even joke about suicide. I couldn't bear to lose somebody else.

Phil/C – Chill babe. I'm just exaggerating. Seriously though. Are they really going to put up another memorial wall next to Casey's? I think everybody is still pissed about what Freddie wrote on hers.

PrincessKirigoe – Yeah, but what does it matter now? Surely people will be sympathetic?

Phil/C – I just think it's asking for trouble. Freddie made a few enemies. He was too much of a joker to have his own memorial wall and for it NOT to get defaced.

PrincessKirigoe – Ugh, if it does, I just don't want to see it.

1010111100 – .

Phil/C – What? Who's that?

PrincessKirigoe – Uh, I don't know.

Phil/C – Has somebody joined our chat?

PrincessKirigoe – Yeah, but they're not on my contact list. Yours?

Phil/C – Nope. A glitch maybe?

PrincessKirigoe – I've never seen anything like that before.

1010111100 – μ 12424¶¶≈Σμ$gg78£%∏®Δ®

Phil/C – What the fuck?

PrincessKirigoe – Check out their profile. Their email address isn't published. No first/last name either.

Phil/C – Hey buddy! Who the fuck are you and how did you join our chat?

PrincessKirigoe – Who is this?

PrincessKirigoe – Who ≥†‡is th556is?

PrincessKirigoe – What the fuck? I didn't write that!

PrincessKirigoe – What th11≠≈   Σe fuck? I didn't write that!

PrincessKirigoe – This is super creepy.

Phil/C – Log off. I'll call you.

Started on Sat May 29 11:23:56 1999

Participants:

Philip Cox – Phil/C

Riley Parker - PrincessKirigoe

PrincessKirigoe – Wakey wakey!

Phil/C – Hey :) I've been up for hours.

PrincessKirigoe – Yeah, right. I know how much of an early riser you are ;-)

Phil/C – I don't sleep much these days. No sign of our mysterious gatecrasher?

PrincessKirigoe – Looks like it's just us. That was so weird.

Phil/C – You find out any more about him after we spoke?

PrincessKirigoe – Their ICQ number looks like binary. I translated it but it's nothing. I also used a program to find their IP address. You can do that if you have their ICQ number. You're not going to believe this …

Phil/C – try me

PrincessKirigoe – Their IP address is the same as mine.

Phil/C – Sooooo, your own computer was fucking with us last night?

PrincessKirigoe – Basically. I don't get it.

Phil/C – You don't think that this is part of that whole hacking thing with Crawdaddy? Have you heard any more about those guys anyway?

PrincessKirigoe – No. Motix21 had gone radio silent. Everybody's keeping their heads down.

Phil/C – Maybe somebody's hacking us?

PrincessKirigoe – That's all I can think of too. But who?

Phil/C – No idea. Feds?

PrincessKirigoe – Don't scare me. It might well be them.

Phil/C – But you haven't done anything wrong. You wiped your hard drive, right?

PrincessKirigoe – Yeah. But I think they're watching me just in case. Ugh, this is so creepy!

Phil/C – Don't get paranoid. There's nobody here right now, right?

PrincessKirigoe – How can we be sure? I don't even know how they invited themselves into our chat last night but I don't think they meant to be visible. Those messages look like accidental glitches.

Phil/C – You don't think Freddie was also mixed up in this whole thing, do you? Is that why he was acting so weird before his death?

PrincessKirigoe – I don't think so. He was too wrapped up in that online girlfriend of his. He would have told me if he was involved with Crawdaddy. He knew we were in contact with him.

Phil/C – Yeah, I know. But it just feels like there's too much weird shit going on right now for it not to be connected.

PrincessKirigoe – I can't stop thinking about Freddie's mysterious girlfriend. Did he tell you anything about her at all?

Phil/C – Only that they had great cybersex.

PrincessKirigoe – Hehe ;-) I'd like some of that right now mister …

Phil/C – I'd prefer the real thing. Your folks home?

PrincessKirigoe – Yeah, but they're going out this evening …

Phil/C – I'll drop by then ;) seven OK?

PrincessKirigoe – Seven is fine :-)

Started on Mon May 31 15:26:06 1999

Participants:

Philip Cox – Phil/C

PrincessKirigoe – Hi

Phil/C – Hi.

PrincessKirigoe – Are you OK? Today was pretty intense …

Phil/C – Yeah. Sorry. Some people just piss me off, that's all.

PrincessKirigoe – You get any shit from Principal Rush?

Phil/C – No. I think he's cutting me some slack because of all that's happened.

PrincessKirigoe – Still, you really beat the crap out of Mike. What did he even say?

Phil/C – Nothing much. Just something about Casey. It set me off. My mind feels like it's gonna explode with all this bad shit. I know something is happening to us but I don't know what it is. There's something that connects Casey and Freddie's deaths and I know it's connected to that weird intruder in our chat the other day. Do we even know that your whole hacker thing was for real? Maybe it was some scam or part of all this. Fuck, I don't know.

PrincessKirigoe – Hey, don't get carried away. There are such things as coincidences.

Phil/C – Look, there's something I haven't told you. I've been seeing things.

PrincessKirigoe – What kind of things?

Phil/C – I don't want to talk about it. Just things. In my room at night. I think I might have whatever Casey had. I'm fucking scared.

PrincessKirigoe – Baby, is this why you've not been sleeping? Come to mine tonight. You know my parents are away again.

Phil/C – Ok thanx. I don't want to be alone right now.

PrincessKirigoe – Maybe you'll get some sleep with me there. Or maybe not ;-) I wouldn't mind recording ourselves again. That was super hot :-)

Phil/C – We're making quite the porno diary heheh :) Maybe we should start selling copies like that Pam and Tommy video.

PrincessKirigoe – Hmm … not sure I want everybody around the world jacking off to us x-D … I think we should just let them have Pam and Tommy.

Phil/C – See you in an hour?

PrincessKirigoe – Sure :-)

Profile of Riley Parker

From *Ghost in the Machine: The Montgomery County Murders* by David Williamson (Tulane University Press: 2001), p. 64:

The Bronsons and the Parkers became friends when Michael Parker hired Mark Bronson to represent him in an architect's liability case. Michael and Mark's friendship developed over the course of the case (which Michael successfully beat in November of 1980), helped no doubt by the fact that their wives were both pregnant with their first children at the same time.

A Maryland native, Michael started his architecture firm in 1975. Yuni Hayashi, a young, Japanese American joined the firm in 1978 and became a full partner and his wife a year later. Riley was born in March, 1981, and Yuni, always the workaholic, was back at her job less than five weeks after Riley's birth. Riley would be the Parkers' only child.

The Parkers and the Bronsons remained close, and their children attended the same kindergarten, elementary, middle school and finally Wakefield High. Riley and Freddie liked each other, and later shared an interest in science fiction and computers.

The atmosphere in the Parker household was sophisticated, business-focused and high achieving. Fortunately, Riley was a smart kid, excelling at school with ease, particularly in math and science, but she was also artistic, drawing cartoons and comics from a young age. Her sense of fashion was colorful, often expressed with brightly printed tank tops and shiny PVC pants. Pink and turquoise animal print featured heavily in her wardrobe and her neon hair regularly alternated between shades of pink, blue and purple.

Riley maintained a close connection to her Japanese heritage. She was an avid fan of the Japanese 'manga' comic book *Sailor Moon* and had large collections of Tamagotchis and Hello Kitty merchandise courtesy of indulgent maternal grandparents in Osaka who regularly sent gifts. The Parkers visited Japan when Riley was five and again when she was twelve and, according to school friends, she couldn't stop talking about that second visit. It had a big effect on her and she reveled in having an 'other' heritage to go with her outsider status. Even the name of her online persona, 'PrincessKirigoe', was taken from *Perfect Blue* (1997); her favorite anime (a Japanese style of animation).

It was online that Riley felt most comfortable. Her interest in anime was not shared by many peers at Wakefield High and she often felt like an outsider. But her discovery of computers and the internet at around the age of fourteen opened a doorway to a new world of online friends with similar interests. She regularly posted on Usenet newsgroups dedicated to anime, manga and PlayStation games.

It was Riley who introduced Freddie Bronson to Usenet and he was immediately hooked. They grew closer than ever before, bonding over website construction (hers, fan sites for the anime series *Mobile Suit Gundam Wing* and *Dragon Ball Z*, his, a potpourri of links to morbid and mysterious online sites as well as links to Usenet files containing his own homemade levels for the video game *Doom*).

At some point in their late-teens, Riley and Freddie became interested in what are now called ARGs (Artificial Reality Games). These games are essentially interactive fictional storylines which unfold on a variety of platforms like online message boards and emails, letters, phone calls and occasionally real-world events like treasure hunts to fully immerse the player in the story. ARGs happen in real time with messages and puzzles released by the creators either according to a schedule or in response to the actions of the players. Theories and solutions are shared by players, creating a collaborative experience.

One of the earliest ARGs was *Ong's Hat* created by Joseph Matheny revolving around the real-life ghost town of Ong's Hat, New Jersey. Beginning in the 1980s with mailed magazine articles, the story of Ong's Hat blurred reality with science fiction and theories about alternate dimensions in its fabrication of a paranormal legend about the town. It utilized the new technology of the internet to spread the legend, drawing in thousands of online players until Matheny was forced to bring it all to a halt in 2001 as more and more people were becoming convinced that it was a real conspiracy theory.

Some of the most popular ARGs fall into the horror genre of storytelling, utilizing their interactive nature to heighten the sense of fear and danger. Players aren't merely witnesses, they are part of the story and their actions have consequences. "It's like those old chainmails," fellow Wakefield High student Dwight Ulrich explains. "But the net has really taken things beyond the old 'if you don't share this email, you'll see a dead girl in your bathroom in the middle of the night' days. These games are really advanced and sometimes you don't even know it's a game until you are already into it."

Could that be what happened in the tragic case of Riley Parker? Did she fail to see the line between game and reality?

The relationship between Freddie and Riley was strained during the last days of their lives with Freddie acting increasingly strange and Riley engaging in a clandestine relationship with Freddie's best friend (and *her* best friend's boyfriend), Phil Cox. Riley and Phil had spent more and more time together in the spring of 1999 and it is unclear when their romantic relationship started. No reference in their online messages points to an instigating incident and they were clearly being careful. By May, Riley had introduced Phil to what she thought was a new online game. But when she started being contacted by a mysterious player called 'Crawdaddy', she began to suspect that it might not be as playful as she had previously thought.

TRANSCRIPT OF POLICE INTERVIEW OF RILEY PARKER (06/01/99)

Tape Recorded Interview

Person Interviewed: Parker, Riley

Date of Interview: 1st June, 1999

Place of Interview: Montgomery Country Police Department

Interviewing Officer(s): Detective Steven Alexander

SA This is Detective Steven Alexander, Montgomery Country Police Department. Today's date is Thursday, May the first, 1999. The time is 9:51 A.M. This will be a taped conversation with the last name of Parker, P-A-R-K-E-R, first of Riley R-I-L-E-Y. Date of birth 08-30-81.

SA Riley, I want to inform you that this interview is being tape recorded. Now, I advised you of your rights earlier, is that not correct?

RP Yes.

SA Speak up, please.

RP Yes.

SA I'd like to go over the events of last night. Philip Cox came to your house at what time?

RP About 9.

SA And Philip was your boyfriend, is that correct?

RP Well ... not exactly. Kind of. It's complicated.

SA How so?

RP He was Casey's boyfriend ... oh God ...

SA I'm aware of that. But after her death, you two hooked up?

RP We hooked up before she died. Jesus ...

SA I see. And what did you and Philip do that evening?

RP We watched a movie and then ... we ... had sex and ...

SA And what?

RP Nothing.

SA Did you film yourselves having sex?

RP Yes.

SA With the webcam, right? Do you do this often?

RP Sometimes. Only twice.

SA And did you and Phil have any kind of fight that night?

RP No. Jesus, I didn't kill him! How many times do I have to say that?

SA Alright, settle down. Now, how about we go over exactly what you do remember. What time did you go to sleep?

RP Eleven, I think. About then.

SA And what time did you wake up?

RP Around seven, I guess.

SA And you don't remember waking up at all during the night?

RP No.

SA And what happened when you woke up?

RP He was just sitting there, in the chair by the door, like he was watching me, but his eyes ...

SA Philip was?

RP Yes ... Oh, God! His face! And the blood! So much blood ...

SA He was dead when you woke up?

RP Yes.

SA You're sure you don't remember anything else from that night?

RP I didn't kill him! It was them! They came for him in the night!

SA Them?

RP FBI or CIA or NSA, take your pick. Whoever is behind it all.

SA Behind what?

RP We were playing a game online, at least, we thought it was a game. But it was some sort of secret transmissions, government stuff, spy stuff, I don't know! But they know that we know and now Phil is dead! Jesus!

SA Settle down, Riley. You're not making much sense, and I need to know how Philip died.

RP I told you, they killed him!

SA Riley, did you leave the webcam recording all night?

RP No. We switched it off when we were done ...

SA You're sure you switched it off?

RP Yes. I think so. Wait. Are you saying my webcam was on all night?

SA It appears that there is a sizable video file on your computer which suggests that it carried on recording through the night, yes.

RP Well then that will prove that I didn't kill Phil! Watch the video! You'll see what really happened!

SA We have an analyst going through your computer files as we speak.

RP Just watch it! I didn't kill Phil! Those guys did, the feds ... don't you get it? Everybody is dead! They're trying to kill us all!

SA Settle down, Riley.

RP I'm not safe here! I'm not safe anywhere! They can get to me wherever I am!

SA I'm going to have to ask you to control yourself, Riley ...

RP Fuck you! You can't protect me! Nobody can!

SA Stop! Sit down!

RP I'm already dead and you can't see it!

End of interview.

EXTRACT OF WEBCAM FOOTAGE ANALYSIS (06/01/99)

Made by: Dr. Kevin Fogg (Forensic Video Analyst for the Montgomery County Police Department)

Date of Recording: 06/01/1999

Time: 22:56 p.m. – 7:22 a.m.

Location: *Address withheld*

Camera: Webcam belonging to Riley Parker

01:38 – Philip Cox begins tossing and turning with more frequency. He seems to be having a troubled sleep.

02:05 – Philip Cox places an arm over Riley Parker's face, and she pushes it away. Neither wake up.

03:22 – Philip Cox gets out of bed. Riley Parker rolls into the spot he vacated and continues sleeping. Philip Cox walks over to the window and stands facing the blinds. His head is lowered, and he appears to be asleep. He remains in this position for over an hour.

03:53 – Riley Parker rolls over. Philip Cox is still by the window.

04:44 – Philip Cox leaves the room. His slow movements suggest that he is sleepwalking.

04:57 – Philip Cox returns to the bedroom. He has what looks like a kitchen knife in his right hand. He approaches the bed and stands over Riley Parker and appears to watch her while she sleeps.

05:17 – Philip Cox leaves the side of Riley Parker and goes to the chair by the bedroom door. He sits down and watches her for a while.

05:32 – Philip Cox raises his right hand and places the blade of the knife against his right eye. Using his left hand, he pulls the eyelid taught and cuts through the skin with the knife. He then does the same with his right eye, letting the severed eyelids fall to the floor. He then puts the knife blade into his mouth and cuts through his right cheek, using a sawing motion, until he almost reaches his right ear. Turning the knife around, he does the same to the left cheek. He then reaches across himself to place the blade of the knife against the left side of his throat. With a slow, controlled movement, he draws the blade across his throat, severing the jugular, carotid arteries, and trachea, and not stopping until he reaches the opposite point on the right side of his throat. Blood pumps from the wound, drenching his white t shirt. His right arm falls limp, and the knife falls to the floor.

05:34 – Philip Cox's head slumps back against the wall. This is his estimated time of death.

06:46 – Riley Parker turns over and continues sleeping, face down.

07:16 – Riley Parker rolls onto her back and her eyes open.

07:18 – Riley Parker sits up in bed and looks in the direction of Philip Cox. She screams and gets out of bed, throwing the covers to one side. She screams again.

PROFILE OF PHILIP COX

From *Ghost in the Machine: The Montgomery County Murders* by David Williamson (Tulane University Press: 2001), p. 42:

Philip Cox was old for his grade and big for his age. Born in 1980, to Steven Cox, an electronics salesman and Heather Cox (née Hewson), a librarian, Phil was an only child in a volatile household. Steven and Heather's marriage had already begun to deteriorate before Phil was born and neighbors report that Steven was a man possessed of a violent temper. When Phil was twelve, his father left the family for good. While that certainly cooled things down in the small house, Heather struggled financially to raise her son.

It resulted in a chip on Phil's shoulder. Most of his friends growing up lived in the more affluent parts of Wheaton and he overcompensated in measuring up to them, making up for any financial shortcomings with a tough-guy attitude and a tendency to avenge any insult with ferocity.

Not every son of a single mother desperately needs a father figure, but in Phil's case, many of his teachers agree that it wouldn't have hurt. Heather had little control over her son who, from the age of fourteen, dwarfed her and he had inherited his father's temper. He came and went as he pleased, knowing that there was little she could do about it.

Phil liked aggressive music like Limp Bizkit and the German industrial metal band Rammstein. He and his best friend, Frederick Bronson, had tickets to the Woodstock '99 festival that summer and it's hard not to imagine them being part of the contingent of troublemakers who made that festival so notorious. From classmate Sarah Wills: "Not to speak ill of the dead or anything, but I just know Phil and Freddie would have been some of those douchebags setting fires and knocking over food trucks at Woodstock '99. They were always out to have a good time and didn't care who got in the way."

And it wasn't just aggressive music that gave Phil a buzz. He and Freddie played violent video games like *Carmageddon, Duke Nukem 3D* and the *Tekken* fighting game series. Phil also shared Freddie's passion for horror movies, though not to the encyclopedic extent of his friend. He wasn't as book smart either, labeled by teachers as a 'classic underachiever' and barely scraped by with a passing grade. He enjoyed better success on the sports field and was on Wakefield High's track and field team, which came second in the state championships in 1999. He was also a keen rollerblader and could often be found at the halfpipe at the local park or 'grinding' on the steps to the youth center.

Phil also had a creative side and his English Lit teacher remarks how focused he could be when he had a story to tell. "He enjoyed English class," George Swanson recalls. "When you could get Phil Cox to settle down and stop horsing around, he could really turn out something good. He had a sense of narrative and a grasp of language which set him above some of his peers. If only he could have seen it for himself, he might not have felt the need to try so hard to impress in less positive ways."

Despite occasional moments where something creative and sensitive shone through, Phil Cox isn't fondly remembered by many at Wakefield High. On two separate occasions, mothers of younger boys wrote to the school to complain about their sons being bullied by Phil. One was a freshman whom Phil allegedly picked on repeatedly, one time throwing his backpack over the high fence of a private property where it snagged on the barbed wire and got stuck there.

Thuggish and unpleasant he may have been at times, there is no denying that Phil was handsome, and he easily earned the attention of his female peers. Casey Jackson is a classic case of the good girl with a thing for bad boys and the two of them were earmarked to be king and queen of the prom that year; an engagement neither of them would live to see. It tells us yet more of Phil's casual disregard for the feelings of others that he was sleeping with her best friend at the time.

What girls like Casey Jackson and Riley Parker see in boys like Phil Cox may be a mystery to most of us but there is no denying that Riley and Phil were a better fit. Both were deeply immersed in more niche and alternative pop culture while Casey, a wholesome girl who was content with *Dawson's Creek* and mainstream music, struggled a little to keep up with the conversation at times. Perhaps it was that Casey was too sweet, too *innocent*, that drove Phil to turn to Riley.

And, although Phil was no IT whizz like Freddie or Riley, he was keen to dabble in the things that excited them. He regularly took command of their small clique, both offline and online. His creative streak was excited when he discovered an online writing contest offering a cash prize for fresh horror stories. Such was Phil's influence over the four friends, that they all apparently submitted stories to the website (which has never been found), hoping to win and split the prize money.

Transcript of Spring Grove Hospital Center Patient Session (06/02/99)

Patient (PT): Riley Parker

Therapist (TH): Dr. Andrew Scully

Date of Session: 06/02/1999

SESSION TEXT

TH Good morning, Riley. How are you feeling today?

PT Better. When can I leave here?

TH Let's not get ahead of ourselves, Riley. We need to find out what's troubling you. Don't you agree?

PT What's troubling me is that government assassins have murdered all my friends and they're going to kill me next.

TH I see. And you don't feel safe here?

PT Phil wasn't safe in my own bedroom. They killed him while I was asleep. They can do anything.

TH And who do you think these people are?

PT I just don't know. Some secret agency. Off the books. Whoever is behind it all.

TH Behind what?

PT I told you about the man who asked us to hack the JPL.

TH The ... uh ... the game? The online game?

PT That's what we thought it was in the beginning. But's it's not a game! It's real! We uncovered something and they killed Phil for it!

TH Why would these people kill Phil?

PT Because we know ... That's why Casey and Freddie are dead too. They're killing us off one by one because we know too much!

TH Listen to yourself, Riley. Philip's face was mutilated. He died through loss of blood from horrific injuries. If silencing Phil was their priority, why not just shoot him? Why the spectacle? And you were left untouched. Why wouldn't these ... uh, agents kill you too if you know as much as Phil did?

PT I don't know! I don't know!

TH All right, Riley calm yourself. Let's look at the facts, huh? And see what theories they support. The fact is, and this cannot be disputed, Phil killed himself in your bedroom. There is footage showing this. Your webcam recorded it all. He got up in the middle of the night, took a knife from downstairs and cut his own throat. I understand the police showed you this footage?

PT He also fucked up his face ...

TH Did they show you the footage, Riley?

PT Yes.

TH Then you know that it wasn't some government agents who came in and killed him, right?

PT That's not how it works ... I'm not talking about men in black shooting you in the back of the head. They are using some special way to kill, so it doesn't look like murder. Something in the internet ...

TH Were Freddie and Casey playing this online game that you and Phil were?

PT No. I don't think they knew anything about it, but they must be connected somehow. Why else would they be dead?

TH I agree.

PT You do?

TH I agree that it is too much of a coincidence that three high school friends end up dead for it not to be connected. But once again, we must look at the facts. Your friend Freddie, I understand, was shot by the police after he tried to kidnap a baby.

PT He was being blackmailed.

TH By whom?

PT We're going around in fucking circles! I told you; I DON'T KNOW!

TH And Casey? Died of a heart attack. Not a mark on her.

PT She was seeing things. Shadows. She was literally scared to death.

TH And that really brings us to the nub of the matter. If Casey was seeing things, then might you and your friends not also be suffering from delusions? Some sort of mass hysteria or a shared psychosis that made Phil kill himself and Freddie endanger the life of an infant? What I want to find out is why. What is the common denominator. Did you and your friends experiment with any drugs in the past six months?

PT No! God, it's not drugs! I've already been through this with my parents. I've never touched drugs and neither did any of the others. It's something we've all been exposed to, something in the internet which messed with our brains, made the others kill themselves in weird ways.

TH But why, Riley. Why go to such lengths just to silence people?

PT I don't know! I don't know!

TH All right, Riley, let's let it rest for now. We'll have another discussion tomorrow. How are you sleeping? Shall I have the nurse give you something?

PT No! I don't want to be medicated! I need my mind clear and sharp because they'll come for me too! I need to be able to trust my senses!

TH All right, Riley, as you say. We'll see how things go over the next few days. But the most important thing I want you to do is rest.

END OF SESSION

BEAUTY IN DARKNESS: THE ONLINE JOURNAL OF CHLOE EVANS (06/05/99)

June 05, 1999

I visited Riley Parker today at Spring Grove today. I know I'm not her friend or anything and I feel a little guilty doing it under false pretenses, but I need to know what the fuck is happening to the students at my school. Most of all, I need to find out what happened to Casey. For the friendship we used to have.

Needless to say, Riley was surprised to see me, but she played along and I don't think the nurses suspected that we barely know each other. Riley looked kind of OK, considering that she was in a mental asylum after recently seeing her boyfriend cut half his face off. There were rumors that she was paranoid about government agencies being behind it. Real X-Files shit and that's why she was put in Spring Grove. I guess what she went through would be enough to make anybody paranoid but with all that happened to Casey, Freddie, and then Phil, then I'm not hasty to throw anybody's theory out. If there is any truth to what she's saying, then that's what I want to find out.

I snuck in a tape recorder as I didn't want to miss anything she said to me. Rather than post the transcript of our conversation, I have written the following in a more digestible form, based on what she and I said to each other. Nothing is made up or exaggerated for dramatic effect.

"Hey, Riley," I said, sitting down as the last of the nurses shut the door, leaving the two of us alone.

"Hey ... Chloe," she replied, as if searching for my name. "You came to visit me?"

"Yeah, I know it's weird," I said. "I just wanted to see you. Everybody's talking about you at school."

"I bet," she replied, scratching at the tabletop with a broken fingernail showing the last remnants of neon green nail varnish. "I'm the last one standing and they put me in the looney bin."

"Nobody knows what to think," I went on. "I mean, we only get little bits of info from the cops. I was wondering ..."

"If I would give you the whole story?" she snapped. "Of how Phil mutilated himself while I slept in the same room?"

I swallowed, recognizing that Riley was on a knife edge. I would have to choose my words carefully. I didn't want her thinking I was some sort of morbid tourist. "None of it makes any sense," I said, "but maybe you know something the papers aren't saying? I mean, people are worried about you ..."

"His face, Chloe, Jesus, you should have seen his face! His mouth was cut into a gross grin! Like, ear to ear! He just sat there, grinning at me and his eyes! Fuck, his eyes! They had no eyelids, and he just sat there staring at me with wide, white eyes and all covered in blood! I can still feel his stare on me!"

She broke down at this point and I was worried her crying would summon the nurses and get me tossed out.

"Why don't you start at the beginning?" I said. "Tell me everything that led to that night. Help me to understand."

"I've been through this with the cops and the doctors more times than I can count," she said, smearing away her tears with the back of her hand. Usually Riley wears almost as much makeup as me (although significantly more colorful), and it was odd seeing her with none, stripped down to her barest core, sitting across the table from me in that sterile room wearing a hospital gown.

"I'm not a cop or a doctor," I said. "I'm just Chloe from school. I know we don't talk much, but I come as a friend. Do you want me to relay your story? So everybody can hear the truth from your lips without it being screened by people who don't believe you?"

"They won't believe me anyway," she said. "But you're right. You can be my mouthpiece." She brightened a little at the notion. "I can reach others through you while I'm kept locked up here. I'm not crazy, Chloe. There is something out there that is dangerous."

"Start at the beginning."

"It began with a game."

"A game?"

"Yeah, one of those online treasure hunts. Code cracking, that sort of thing. There was a post on Usenet from somebody claiming to be looking for highly intelligent individuals for an unknown task. To find them, they had devised a series of tests. The first test was part of the original post itself. Beneath the message, there was a binary sequence which, when translated into plain text, looked like gibberish. It was another user, a guy called Motix21, who figured out that it needed decoding further and, by using a simple shift code, we were able to figure out that it was a URL."

"And that took you to the next clue?" I asked.

"Yeah. The website was just a simple page with a video. It was one of the most unsettling videos I've ever seen. It was just shots of empty, abandoned places like parking lots, swimming pools and shopping malls intercut with footage of a woman being tortured. It was really disturbing, and we all thought it might be something real like it was filmed by a serial killer or something. Footage from a snuff movie, you know? It was Phil who identified the torture scenes as clips from a movie called *Videodrome*. He didn't recognize the other clips and neither did Freddie."

"You brought Freddie in on this?"

"Only to help identify the source of the footage. He wasn't really interested in playing the game. He was too wrapped up in that new girlfriend of his."

"Go on."

"So, we figured that the inserts from *Videodrome* might have been put there to confuse us. By removing them, we could just focus on the shots of abandoned places and look for clues there. While we were able to identify a couple of the locations, we really weren't any closer to solving the puzzle until we focused on the sound. There was a low buzzing which alternated in frequency along with some weird bell chiming. It was Motix21 who had the idea to turn the sound file into a spectrogram."

"A visual representation of sound?"

"Yeah. You can turn any image into sound and that's what the puzzle was. By converting the audio into an image, Motix21 came up with a simple black square with another URL. We all rushed to the website, but it just showed an image of an empty cardboard box. It was like whoever made it was taunting us, leaving clues and then deliberately sending us down a dead end. Motix21 thought that maybe a message would be hidden in the image itself, so he tried running it through a steganography program."

"A what?"

"Steganography is like looking for messages hidden inside other media. In the digital age it's basically encrypted data within the code of the object itself. I don't completely get it but Motix21 was able to extract a message which simply said; "I am God"."

"That's ... a little creepy."

"Yeah, no shit. We thought we had all been taken for a giant ride and that the game was over. We were pretty pissed but then, we got the phone calls."

"Phone calls?"

"Don't ask me how he knew our landline numbers because I still don't know. He must have known our identities even then because how else could he call us? It should have made us all way more creeped out than it did, but we were just so hyped that the game was still on and that we had been selected for the next stage. It really felt like we were the chosen ones, you know?"

"The phone calls ...?"

"Right. It was just some girl's voice reading a bunch of numbers and letters. An automated message like they use on numbers stations. You've heard of those, right?"

"Sure. Spies use them for sending encrypted messages via radio, right?"

"Right. So, we had another code to crack. Motix managed it in a couple of hours. It was a hexadecimal sequence which, when decoded, provided yet another URL. The website was just a black screen with a message from the game's creator; somebody called Crawdaddy2281, who claimed to be some sort of hacker who was recruiting smart people online to help him with a task. Crawdaddy used to work for the JPL and was kicked out for asking too many questions about some mysterious transmissions received from the Galileo satellite. Aliens, presumably. Anyway, he needed our help in breaking into the JPL server. He said there was information there that would blow everybody's mind."

"But this was all part of the game, right?" I said. "I mean … aliens …"

"It was no game," Riley said. "Crawdaddy was onto something and they arrested him."

"Who did?"

"The government, I guess. Some coverup or something. I don't know what he was charged with but he found out too much and they put him away. We all backed off after that. I mean, if a super hacker like Crawdaddy could get busted then what chance did any of us have? We didn't know it then, but it was already too late."

I didn't know what to say to all this. It really seemed like Riley had lost the ability to tell the difference between the game and reality. I tried to reason with her. "How do you know that this Crawdaddy didn't spread rumors of his own incarceration? Maybe it's part of the game to keep you guessing?"

"And Phil? And Freddie? And Casey?" She was getting agitated now, her voice rising.

"What makes you think their deaths are connected?" I asked.

"How can they not be? It's something *in* the internet, some code or website we were all exposed to. You've heard of subliminal messages? Stuff that flashes in front of your eyes so quickly that you don't take it in on a conscious level. Only your subconscious does."

"Sure. Like backmasking in heavy metal music ..."

"Yeah, I guess."

(I was humoring her. The whole backmasking thing has been pretty much debunked as a myth cooked up by the religious right).

"I think we all received some subliminal signal from the net," she went on, "which made us all a bit crazy. Casey was seeing shadows and I'm pretty sure that was what was pursuing her the night she died. She was terrified the last few days of her life and I should have listened to her. She tried to tell me that something was wrong, but ... well, because I was sleeping with Phil and all ... I just felt too guilty to speak with her much. Did you know she was sleeping in her treehouse before she died because she was too scared to sleep in her room?"

(That comment set some alarm bells ringing in my head, which I'll get around to shortly).

"And Freddie?" I asked. "He was acting pretty weird too, but it was the cops that shot him, not some weird affliction."

"Yeah, but there's more to that," she said. "His sister told me that he was also living in fear of somebody or something. She thought somebody was blackmailing him, making him do crazy things or she'd reveal something about him. I don't know. Somebody had to have got to him for him to kidnap a fucking baby. And then Phil ..."

She got distant at that point, like her mind was drifting off on purpose, not wanting to dwell on it.

"Was he acting weird before he died?" I asked. "I didn't exactly know him well ..."

"He wasn't sleeping, I know that much," she said. "And he said he was seeing things in his room late at night, just like Casey did. Yeah, he was acting weird. They all were. And now I'm in the nut house. I'm scared of what's going to happen to me! I know too much!"

"Listen, Riley," I said. "Casey wasn't playing the game. And Freddie only helped you with one of the clues."

"I know, I know!" she bawled. "They had nothing to do with it but somehow they all got caught up in it and it's my fault!" I caused their deaths!"

She was yelling now, and this was the last straw for the nurses. They came marching in, their eyes spitting fire at me. "All right, now that's quite enough for today," one of them said. "You're going to have to leave."

My time was up. While the nurses tried to calm Riley and called for the doctor, I made my exit. I had more than enough for my mind to chew over in any case.

Riley is messed up in the head, there is no doubt about that. She thinks she was within a whisker of talking to aliens before some government agency started arresting people and driving others mad. It might all have been a game and Riley doesn't know how to stop playing. I don't know what happened to Casey and Freddie and

Phil, but there has to be a connection somewhere. I'm just not sure it's the connection Riley thinks it is.

The only kind of lead our conversation gave me was what Riley had told me about Casey during her final days. She said that she had been sleeping in her treehouse. Now, that treehouse was something Casey's dad had built when we were in fifth grade, back when we were best friends. We had loved that thing and I haven't thought about it in years. It was our little hideaway. We'd sneak stuff in there from the house; candy, potato chips and stuff and hide them in a little space under a floorboard we had prised loose. When we were a little older, we also hid letters and poems we wrote to boys we had crushes on but never had the guts to send them.

Tomorrow I'm going to visit Casey's parents and see if I can't get a look inside that treehouse. I don't know if I'll find anything and it's going to be super awkward after all these years, but I have to try. I still have so many questions.

Until tomorrow, gothlings. Stay dark and beautiful. \m/

PROFILE OF CHLOE EVANS

From *Ghost in the Machine: The Montgomery County Murders* by David Williamson (Tulane University Press: 2001), p. 72:

Chloe Evans was only peripherally connected to the core group of teenagers who died so mysteriously in the summer of 1999, but she placed herself there voluntarily. Always the outsider, Chloe could have remained apart from it all. Her heavy, black makeup and her alignment with the 'goth' subculture dictated that she play the part of the morbidly detached and cynical outcast. But she didn't. It was her friendship with Casey Jackson which drove her from the shadows and back into the uncomfortable light of day, if only for a while.

Chloe befriended Casey in the fifth grade. Always a shy girl, Chloe reached out to the newly arrived Casey and the two of them hit it off from the get-go. Casey, bubbly and outgoing was a perfect match for the more introverted Chloe who had always felt out of sync with her peers and occasionally suffered from bullying.

Cynical minds might interpret her befriending of Casey as a defense mechanism to shield herself from further torment but that doesn't explain the fact that the girls liked each other and remained friends for much of middle school.

When Chloe was twelve, tragedy struck. Her mother died from cancer, leaving Chloe and her father, Roger Evans, to take care of each other. From an early age, Chloe took over many of the household chores like laundry and cooking as Roger worked long hours as a machinist in a factory. The two of them lived a modest existence in a small house in Glenmont Forest and neighbors said that Chloe seemed to parent her father rather than the other way around as he would frequently turn to the bottle to drown his sorrows amid bouts of deep depression.

The death of her mother inevitably made Chloe retreat even further into herself and her outlook on life grew irrevocably daker. Her dress sense turned to black and her makeup grew thicker, almost corpselike, as if it were a black and white death mask to hide behind. The goth scene was a refuge for her and when she wasn't shopping at Hot Topic, she was going to see acts like Marilyn Manson, HIM and Nine Inch Nails, driving her dad's rusty 1991 Dodge Dynasty to concerts in Washinton, Baltimore and even as far as Philadelphia.

It wasn't a scene shared by many at Wakefield High but the prospect of alienating herself even further from her peers did little to discourage Chloe. She decided long ago that she didn't require their approval and had hardened herself to the barbed insults and scathing looks her new fashion sense inevitably earned. Most of the other kids knew to keep their distance in any case. In her freshman year at Wakefield High, Chloe got into a fight with another girl who had apparently picked on her. The other girl had to be taken to hospital to be treated for concussion while Chloe was suspended for a week.

Chloe's descent into darkness marked the end of her friendship with Casey who was the antithesis of whatever it means to be goth. Casey was a ray of sunshine compared to Chloe and seeing the two of them together was like looking at a yin-yang symbol. The pair had a fight at some point before the end of middle school and ended up never speaking again. Casey found new friends in high school while Chloe was apparently content to be a loner, moving through the noisy hallways like a black shadow, keeping to herself, knowing that nobody else would 'get' her interests.

Rebellious and anti-social she may have been, Chloe was also bookish and generally a straight A student. Like many teenagers of her generation, she developed a keen interest in computers and hung out on 'hacker' Usenet groups and IRC channels as much as ones related to the goth scene. She was involved with several hacking operations with various individuals who shared python codes and how-to files. It was never anything too malicious or illegal, mostly mischievous pranks simply because they could. They'd hack into websites belonging to extreme religious or political organizations and mess with their content.

Chloe's own website, 'Beauty in Darkness' was a deeply personal collection of ruminations on the world and cynical commentaries on current affairs in which she also discussed goth culture, hacking and dating. When it came to boys, she struggled to find any on her wavelength. Boys from Wakefield High were decidedly out and she looked further afield for likeminded souls, using the internet to hook up with people. She even took the risk of meeting some of them in person, if they lived close enough, but none made a big enough impression to really become part of her life. She would regularly spill the details of various dates in her journal, occasionally bemoaning the lack of decent men on the scene.

When Casey died mysteriously in May of 1999, Chloe's online journal took a sudden turn for the investigative. Her website was supposed to be anonymous, but Chloe perhaps foolishly used real names and it can't have been hard for her fellow students to uncover her identity. A deluge of vitriolic comments in her guestbook unmasked her and criticized her for attempting to capitalize on the deaths of kids who weren't even her friends. Chloe, in her usual stubbornness, ignored them and continued her investigation, determined to find out what had happened to her former friend, Casey.

Beauty in Darkness: The Online Journal of Chloe Evans (06/06/99)

June 06, 1999

Well, today was fruitful. More fruitful than I could possibly have imagined.

I turned up at the Jackson home at around one this afternoon. They were predictably shocked to see me after all these years, but Mrs. Jackson, bless her, took me straight into the kitchen and got me something to drink. She's in the middle of mourning but still plays the perfect hostess, just like she always used to do. It made me feel even more guilty about the clandestine nature of my visit.

Mr. Jackson appeared and shook my hand and then vanished back into the den, apparently unable to face visitors. Bobby was somewhere upstairs gaming. Mrs. Jackson and I sat at the kitchen table and talked for a while. It was so weird, like I had stepped back in time, and was in seventh grade again. I can't remember how many times I've sat at that table, having dinner with the Jacksons. The kitchen seemed exactly as I remembered it. It had been my home from home during my own mourning. Now it was their turn to grieve.

She seemed touched that I would come to pay my respects even though Casey and I hadn't been friends for a few years. Yeah, that was the bullshit story I fed her. I was there to 'pay my respects'. Ugh! I felt like such a bitch lying to her, but I guess I did my best to make good on my claim and we chatted for about half an hour about Casey and shared a few memories which nearly had us both bawling.

"I know we didn't hang out much after middle school," I said. "But I miss her."

"Oh, we all do," she said. "Casey was a bright light in many lives. Do you want to see her room?"

"Actually, I'd kind of like to see that old treehouse we used to play in," I said. "We spent more time in there than in her room back when we were kids."

"Of course," she said, with a small smile. "Casey was quite attached to that old thing, right up until ... You know, she took to sleeping in it during her final days? I don't know why. Maybe she just wanted the comfort of her memories with you ..."

She teared up again and I didn't know where to look. We shuffled out from behind the table, and she let me out the back door, closing it softly behind her, presumably so she could go and cry in private. I glanced up the length of the back yard to where the treehouse clung to the trunk of a large sycamore, yet more memories rushing back to choke me.

I made my way up to it. It was a pretty good treehouse, even though its planks were showing some green now and the roof had warped a little. I remembered the smell of fresh sawdust the day Casey's dad had finished it and wondered (not for the first time recently) how so much time could pass in seemingly the blink of an eye.

The door creaked open as I pulled on the latch and peered in. It was still cozy inside, filled with a few remnants of our days together. A little potted plant hung from some twine, its occupant long since dried up and dead. A battered old cardboard box in the corner held old issues of teen magazines we used to read together. If Casey had been sleeping here before her death, then there was no sign of it, and I guessed her parents had brought in her sleeping bag and roll mat.

I got down on my hands and knees and began feeling about for the loose floorboard. I couldn't remember exactly which one it was, just that it was in the far-left corner. After some prodding about, I eventually found it and was able to prise up the corner.

Down in the cavity (which still held some sawdust) I could see a book and my heart began to leap as the thought of a diary occurred to me. Had Casey really kept a secret diary in here? I pulled it out and riffled through it.

I was right. It *was* a diary, started sometime last year and, by checking the final entry, I could see that she had continued writing in it until her death. A fucking gold mine! The cops, even her parents didn't know about this, and I might be holding in my hand the final clue that can solve the mystery of what the hell is going on.

Now, I know I should have brought that diary straight to Casey's parents. It's theirs by right and may be the last thing their daughter ever wrote. But I just knew I had to have my time with it first. Once her parents have it, they'll turn it over to the police and then we might never know the truth. If Riley is at all right about some government coverup, then evidence needs to be treated very carefully.

It really wasn't a cool thing to do, but I hid the diary under my sweater and left the treehouse to make my excuses to Casey's parents. I told them that I had done what I had come to do (no lie there) and that I wanted to go home and think about Casey some more. They seemed to buy it and I made tracks.

But this fucking diary!

I've started reading it and am over halfway. I just know that it will contain some answers. Casey, like Riley was seriously messed up and I need to find out what connects them. I WILL get this back to Casey's parents when I'm done with it and tell them that we need to take it to the police. I don't know how I'll explain my taking it from the treehouse without their permission, but I'll think of something. They need to know the truth of what their daughter was going through. The world needs to know the truth.

I will finish reading the diary tonight and make more plans. Look here for an update.

Stay dark and beautiful, gothlings. Answers are coming \m/

Casey Jackson's Diary

The following excerpts are taken from the diary of Casey Jackson which was provided to the police by Chloe Evans after Casey's death. It has been verified by Jackson's parents as genuine.

April 18, 1999

Dear Diary,

Phil and I are going to the lake tonight. He's picking me up soon, so I'd better write quickly. He says he's packing a tent in the back of his pickup so we can camp, if only for a few hours. It's going to be so romantic! I think he wants to make it up to me after taking me to see Carrie 2 last weekend. God that movie sucked! I know he regrets not agreeing to my choice of The Matrix, But honestly, it was kind of funny to watch a really bad movie together. I actually had a really good time, though I'm not telling Phil that. We laughed so much! I'll catch The Matrix another time. I know Riley is desperate to see it.

I have to wrap this up as Phil should be here any minute. I'll let you know how tonight goes. I'm so looking forward to it!

Love, Casey

April 18, 1999 (continued)

Dear Diary,

The lake was awesome! We did the dirty in the tent as soon as we got there (natch) and then we drank beer and watched the sun set over the trees while we talked and talked until it got dark and we had to head home. I really love Phil, I can't even describe to you how much!

On the way home he told me about some online contest he and Freddie are going nuts over. Write a short, scary story and you can win 10,000 dollars! They have this hairbrained idea to enter as a group and then split the winnings. Riley's also onboard and Phil wants me to write something too. He kept telling me that the more people who enter, the bigger the chance is that we'll win. I kept telling him that the more people who enter, the more he has to share the winnings with, but I don't think he really gets it, the big dummy! But he and Freddie are deadly serious over it. They're talking about us all signing an actual contract to make sure the winner doesn't make off with all the money.

I told Phil I'll think about it. And I am. It's not that I really care about the money, but it sounds like fun. And I have the perfect idea for a story kicking around inside my sick head (evil cackle!). I'll let you know how I get on.

Love, Casey

April 19, 1999

Dear Diary,

Phil and Freddie were still talking about the short story contest at school today. I'd forgotten all about it, but their enthusiasm rekindled my interest and I made a start right after school, even before doing any studying. I know it's probably a dumb time to start writing a story when I should be studying for my finals, but I just can't help it. The guys' enthusiasm is infectious. They're so funny! They both refuse to tell the other what their story is about, scared that they'll get ripped off, but they can't help talking all about it. Predictably, they're both writing gorefests.

Riley is more tight-lipped than Phil and Freddie and I wonder what her story is about. It'll probably be some sci-fi thing, but I know she's got a great imagination with all the Japanese stuff she watches.

I wish Freddie and Riley would hook up. They'd be so cute together! Then we'd be able to go on double dates instead of just hanging out as a group of friends. It would be perfect. But Riley told me that it would be weird as they've been friends all their lives. Phil says Freddie says the same thing. I guess they have a point, after all. Imagine dating somebody you remember pissing their pants in kindergarten! I'm just glad I didn't know Phil until high school otherwise we might never have gotten together.

My own story is going to be a little more subtle than Phil's or Freddie's, but I'm still going to have some gore in it. I know Phil would like that. It gives me a small tingle of excitement to think that he might read my story eventually and that just makes me more determined to write something really good.

A little bit more now, and then I HAVE to start studying!

Love, Casey

April 20, 1999

Dear Diary,

My story is coming along nicely. I never knew I had it in me to actually sit down and write something just from my own imagination. I used to quite enjoy writing stories for English class, but this is completely different. There's so much freedom in just writing for yourself (well, and at a chance of getting a share in 10,000 dollars, but you know what I mean!). I'm really pleased with what I've written. It's super creepy! I just hope Phil will like it ...

Love, Casey

April 21, 1999

Dear Diary,

I was going to wait until it was finished, but I just can't help it, I have to tell you a little bit about my story because I'm just so darned proud of it!

It's about a girl who finds a creepy journal online which claims to be written by a serial killer. She thinks it's fake of course, until she realizes that he is describing actual murders ... and posting about them before they happen!

I want to put more gore into it to make it appeal to Phil but I'm trying to figure out how. It's kind of hard to do that when the story is about stuff somebody reads online. I guess I could elaborate on the murders more. It feels kind of sick writing about death and torture but it's only a story after all and it's not like the net isn't full of gross stuff anyway. That sick shit Freddie showed us on that Rotten.com site still haunts me ...

I must get back to writing.

Love, Casey

April 22, 1999

Dear Diary,

Grrrrrrrrrr! I am so angry with myself right now. It's after midnight and I've spent practically the whole evening retyping my story. It was coming along so nicely but I decided to change it from third person to first person. I had made up a character called Laura as my protagonist but it just felt too far removed to be scary enough. I wanted to tell the story from a narrator's perspective to make it hit harder, as if I was telling the reader the story myself. That meant re-writing the whole thing. I thought it would be easy, just switch 'Laura' to 'I', right? Wrong! I had to change the grammar in practically every sentence, and it took hours and I didn't get ANY studying done. Worst of all, I made no progress with the actual story, just spent all night making more work for myself.

My fingers ache from typing and I'm so tired. I can't write any more.

Casey

April 23, 1999

Dear Diary,

Today I feel much better about my story. Yesterday I was ready to delete the whole thing in frustration but I was just tired. Now, having reconstructed it as a first-person narrative, I am into it once again and have made good progress, despite going to the movies after school with Phil, Riley and Freddie (we finally got to see The Matrix and it was AWESOME!)

I figured out an ending for my story and even amped up the blood content to keep gore hounds like Phil happy. It's going to be awesome and might even win! I know it's silly to think that, but hey, a girl's got to have confidence, right?

It's nearly eleven now, and I just wanted to write you a little note before I get back to my story. Dad just knocked on my door and told me to go to bed, but the deadline is approaching and I want to get another hour of writing in.

More tomorrow,

Love, Casey

P.S. Just wait for the final line of the story. It's going to be a KILLER!

April 24, 1999

Dear Diary,

My story is nearly finished! Mom and Dad took Bobby to King's Dominion today and, ordinarily I would have wanted to come with them, but I said I had a lot of studying to do. Even dad was suspicious, and I feel bad about lying to them, but I NEED to get this story finished. The deadline is Monday! Anyway, I got some studying done too, so it wasn't a total lie.

I called Phil to see how close he is to finishing his, but he seemed distracted, like he didn't want to talk. I guess he's pretty stressed about the deadline too. If only he'd put as much effort into his schoolwork! God, I sound like his mom, but seriously, once we've submitted these stories, we really need to knuckle down for our finals. I've really neglected my own studying while I've been writing this story but it's so consuming and I'm really proud of it. I wish I could tell it to you, Diary, but no way am I writing that all out by hand in this little book. I'd use up all the pages!

Anyway, back to the grindstone and then ... STUDY!

Love, Casey

April 25, 1999

Dear Diary,

It's done. My story is done!

Bed now.

Love, Casey

April 26, 1999

Dear Diary,

Today we all submitted our stories to the website. I feel suddenly relaxed, like a great weight has been lifted from my shoulders, which is weird because I still have a ton of studying for my finals coming up. I guess writing it took more out of me than I knew but it was so enjoyable. Who knows? Maybe I have a writer's career ahead of me. Stephen King, watch out!

But I also feel kind of sad that it's over. My story is gone. Taken from me and sucked up into the void of the web. God help it and whoever reads it, please be kind!

Something weird happened online tonight, just before I logged off to write to you. I was talking to Phil on ICQ and for a few minutes, everything I wrote got copied and sent as a second message, just below the one I typed. Phil started teasing me and asking why I kept repeating myself, but I wasn't! It lasted for a few minutes and then went back to normal. Some weird bug in ICQ, I guess.

Love, Casey

Dear Diary,

Today Phil and I had our first fight. It was so stupid but I've been crying pretty much nonstop since it happened. I went over to his after school to study. Usually we mostly make out but I always insist on doing some studying at least. I mean, Phil's not exactly excelling at school and he really needs to pass these finals so I thought I was doing him a favor.

Well, this time he flat out didn't want to stop making out. It was getting close to when I had to go home for dinner and we hadn't opened a single book. He got mad that I kept pulling away from him saying that we should study and then I guess I got mad that he just wanted to make out. He said some really mean things about how I was 'going frigid' on him and I just left.

He called me about an hour ago and we made up after much talking. So much for studying for our finals. First that story competition and now this ... But I love him so much, I couldn't bear it if we broke up.

Love, Casey

P.S. With the fight and all, I almost forgot to tell you I had a super weird dream last night. I was in the bathroom of our old house. I don't know what I was doing back there but I was trying to brush my hair but my reflection in the mirror was just a black smudge. I couldn't make out my own face and then I got really freaked out, thinking that it wasn't even my reflection I was looking at. I got more and more panicked when I started wondering who it might be looking back at me through the mirror that I woke up sweaty and scared. I guess it's because I got so into writing my story last week, it messed me up in the head a little. Whatever. I just hope I don't have any more like that. It was seriously freaky.

April 29, 1999

Dear Diary,

Another weird thing on the internet today. That repeating bug where everything I said got copied? It was back again, only for a few minutes but it got super weird. I was talking to that guy called Mark in Atlanta I told you about. We're just penpals, nothing flirty. Phil doesn't know about him, and I don't think I should tell him. He'd only get the wrong impression. Anyway, we were chatting, and that same thing started happening. Everything I wrote got copied. Super frustrating and I had to explain to Mark that I was experiencing technical problems and then, of course, my explanation got repeated.

It got weirder when my messages started being copied wrong. It started with little spelling errors and missed punctuation. Then, weird symbols started appearing. I can't remember them so I can't write them down here, but it was just about every weird symbol you can find on the keyboard as well as some stuff I've never seen before, peppering the sentences like doodles and breaking up the words. Pretty soon the messages were just gibberish.

I previously thought it was a bug in ICQ, but this time it happened in a Yahoo chatroom. How can two programs have the same bug? Maybe it's my computer? I need to remember to get Riley to take a look at it. I may have a virus.

Love, Casey

April 30, 1999

Dear Diary,

My dreams are getting worse. I woke up in the middle of the night (or, at least, I thought I did) and I couldn't move. I was lying in my bed completely paralyzed and all I could do was move my eyes left and right. I could breathe but it was heavy and labored.

My room was so dark and all I could make out was the edge of my bookcase in the light from the street outside. The corner of the room was a black shadow, blacker than a shadow in fact, and my eyes were drawn to it as if it were a void. I don't know why, but I felt like it shouldn't exist in my dark room of normal nighttime shadows. There was something unnatural about it.

Then, and I don't know if this really happened or if it was my mind, the shadow seemed to change shape. Before I realized it, I was staring at the figure of a man in a long black coat, with a brimmed hat on his head, standing in the corner of my room!

I was so scared. I tried to cry out, but I still couldn't move a muscle. My throat could only make this low, gurgling sound. I honestly thought I was going to die and my hand is shaking as I write this, thinking about how real it felt.

Eventually, I was able to move my fingers and toes and soon the rest of my body. I sat up in bed, but the shadowy figure was gone.

I'm scared to go to sleep tonight because I don't want the same thing to happen. What the hell was it?

Stay by my side, Diary.

Casey

May 1, 1999

Dear Diary.

No dreams last night. Must have just been a passing thing, thank God.

I'm going out for pizza with Phil and the others in a bit, so I must rush. More later, if I have time.

Love, Casey

May 4, 1999

Dear Diary,

I'm sorry I haven't written in a couple of days. Things were going really well between me and Phil and I've been so busy with studying that I just haven't had much free time. But today something really creepy happened to me and I just have to write it down. If I make it real then maybe I won't feel like I'm going crazy. It only happened an hour or so ago and my heart is still racing as I write this.

It's already late but I just had to get this down before I go to bed. I was chatting with the guys on ICQ like usual. Riley and I are the only ones who have webcams and it feels a little icky to be broadcasting my face to the others when they can't show me theirs, but if Riley does, then so do I. It's sort of an unwritten rule between us.

Anyway, the others logged off about an hour ago. I was fooling around with my webcam for a while, taking pictures of me doing cute faces etc. when I caught a glimpse in the feed of something over my right shoulder. It looked like a person standing in the corner of my room.

I turned around and there was nobody there. I looked back at the screen and could definitely see the figure of a man all in black with a brimmed hat, just like in my dream! I kept checking behind me, trying to figure out what the webcam was picking up. There was a shadow in the corner of my room but that was all. Somehow the webcam was making it look like a person.

Really freaked out now, I turned the webcam off and then on again, hoping it was some sort of glitch. This time, there was no figure. Just the shadow between the bookcase and the wall, like normal. He'd gone. I'm certain he was there, though. I had definitely seen the figure of a man and he was wearing a hat. Nothing else about him was discernable. It was the figure from my dream a few nights ago. Why am I seeing him in real life now?

Casey

May 5, 1999

Dear Diary,

The dreams are back again. Big surprise after I was seeing Him in my PC monitor last night.

I woke up and couldn't move again. He was standing in the corner of my room like before, just watching me. I can't see his eyes and I'm glad I can't, but I don't know what he wants and I'm scared. I turned on my webcam today and didn't see anything, but I didn't dare try it this evening. Maybe he only comes at night? I'm dreading seeing Him again. I know it's probably all in my mind but I just want my mind to be OK.

Casey

May 8, 1999

Dear Diary.

I think Phil is cheating on me.

The last couple of nights, I haven't been able to get hold of him. He hasn't been online and isn't answering his cellphone when I call him. I spoke to him about it yesterday and he started acting all weird and saying that I was being too possessive and that he felt smothered. I was scared of having another fight, so I let it drop but something's not right. He's hiding something.

Same story last night. I tried his house and his mom said he was skating at the halfpipe. I tried his cellphone again and he answered at last, but he didn't sound like he was at the halfpipe. It sounded like he was indoors and he seemed a little out of breath. He was pretty snappy with me, like I was interrupting something but he wouldn't say what.

I spoke to Riley about it today as she's basically my best friend, but she told me I was being paranoid. She doesn't think Phil would cheat on me. Am I being paranoid? I keep examining every conversation Phil and I have had over the past few weeks, looking for evidence like a police detective. One minute I convince myself that it is nothing and the next I am back to thinking that there is somebody else.

No more dreams for the past few nights now. I haven't seen any shadows in my webcam feed either. I hope it was all just a trick of my mind, but it doesn't fill me with confidence that I am being rational. I wish I knew what was real and what wasn't!

Love, Casey

Phil is still acting off with me. I've tried to think rationally but it's clear that something is up, even if he isn't seeing someone else. I'm just acting like everything is normal until something tells me for sure if he's cheating.

I feel like the world's biggest liar. People think I'm this goody-two-shoes perfect, grade-A student but only I know that it's all a front. Well, Phil knows too, I guess, but he doesn't really register it. He can be so dumb sometimes. If people only knew the awful things that my mind conjures up! Of how my mind feels like it is cracking apart, seeing things in shadows that aren't there.

A Place of Hurt was born in the mind of this seemingly perfect all-American girl. Part of me wants everybody to know what I'm capable of but part of me is terrified of them finding out. So, I walk through school hallways like an angel but inside I feel like I'm going to explode!

Casey

May 11, 1999

Dear Diary,

The dreams are back.

I woke up at 2:35, I know that because I saw my alarm clock and wasn't able to get back to sleep. The Hat Man was in my room again. I've started calling him that because that's the only discernable thing about him. That creepy wide-brimmed hat.

He was standing in the corner, like before, between the bookcase and the wall and this time he moved. I lay there frozen while he drifted closer to me, not walking exactly, but sort of floating. I couldn't see his legs, they just merged with the rest of the shadows in the room. Luckly, I woke up just as he reached the foot of my bed.

What does he want? What would he do if I didn't wake up in time?

Casey

May 12, 1999

Dear Diary,

It's not in my head.

I recorded the Hat Man on my webcam.

I didn't have any dreams last night so I figured that things were getting better. I haven't used my webcam much recently because I've been too scared that I'll see Him. But this afternoon, the sun was shining in through my blinds and the whole world felt fresh and beautiful with no shadows. So I turned it on and played around with it for a while.

I didn't see him at first (and I looked) and I don't know exactly when He appeared. I just noticed him after a while and I don't know how long He had been watching me.

It was like before; the shadow in my webcam feed looked like a tall, thin, man wearing a hat but when I looked behind me, I couldn't see him. I don't know why he comes and goes or only shows up in my dreams and webcam but this time I was determined to record him. That way I would have proof that I wasn't just imagining things.

I started recording the feed and kept my eyes on the shadow. After a couple of minutes, the shadow seemed to flicker. I watched as it wavered about a bit and then went still. I glanced behind me and saw nothing and when I looked back at my monitor, He was gone.

I spoke to Riley about it on ICQ, well, tried to anyway. I sent the clip of the webcam feed so she could see it herself, but she thought it was just the poor quality of the video making it look like the shadows were moving. I told her about my dreams and about how I feel there is some sort of presence in my room at night, but she said she had to log off because her parents were having friends over.

She doesn't seem like she really wants to talk to me much these days ever since I told her I thought Phil was cheating on me. Whatever. I don't know what her problem is. It's like she thinks I'm making it up for attention or something. First Phil and now this.

I don't know who else to talk to about it. I'm so scared.

Tonight, I'm sleeping in the treehouse. I don't care if my parents think I'm being childish. I can't sleep in my room knowing that He is there.

Casey

May 13, 1999

Things are worse.

The Hat Man is with me wherever I go, even in my waking moments.

I was in the computer lab at school this afternoon, trying to finish my English Lit project. I had been working pretty effectively for about an hour when Sarah Wills came over to me looking pissed. "What the fuck, Casey?" she said.

Everybody looked at us and I didn't know what was going on. Sarah was mad about some messages she thought I had sent her on our school's stupid IM service. I hadn't sent any. She didn't believe me and called me a freak before leaving in a huff. I still had no clue what she was going on about.

So I checked my message history.

There were a bunch of messages between Sarah and me that I had played no part in. Apparently, we had been chatting for most of the hour and I hadn't got any notifications at all. It was like somebody had taken over my account had had continued a full conversation with Sarah while pretending to be me. It was super creepy. They had started by asking her a question about English Lit. She had answered and the conversation had carried on from there.

But 'my' messages were filled with spelling and grammatical errors as well as weird symbols just like those mirrored messages on ICQ. It was the same shit. This bug or whatever it is was now showing up on a school computer which is super weird.

Gradually 'my' messages became more or less indecipherable with long strings of numbers amid phrases that didn't make any sense.

"Everything OK with your keyboard?" Sarah had asked me with a little smiley face.

My answer had been a full paragraph of gibberish except for a very clear sentence amid the nonsensical symbols and glyphs. It said; "Do you want to die, BITCH?" It was the last message between us and that's when Sarah had come over to me.

I got up and hurried out of the lab. People turned to look at me. I think they thought I was going to hurl or something. All I wanted to do was get away from my computer and cry. I ran into the bathroom and sat down in a stall and locked the door. I cried for about ten minutes because I was so scared and didn't know what to do. I still don't. It was no wonder Sarah had got pissed at me and I had no way to prove that it wasn't me sending those messages.

I was sitting there trying to compose myself when I heard somebody come into the bathroom. Their footfalls were heavy and echoing and they didn't sound like a woman's feet. It sounded like a man had walked into the bathroom. I called out, 'Hello?' but they didn't answer.

They opened the stall next to mine and locked it behind them. I could see the shadow of their feet beneath the wall of the stall but not their actual feet. I called out again, wishing they would just answer me but again they stayed silent. There was no other noise.

I got really freaked out sitting there so I left the stall and went over to the washbasin to clean myself up. In the mirror, I could see the door of the stall next to the one I had left slowly start to open, creaking on its hinges. I turned around, my heart hammering, and saw that there was nobody there. There never had been anybody there. But something had come in and now it had gone.

I just can't escape the notion that it was Him.

Casey

May 14, 1999

Dear Diary,

The worst dream yet. I slept in my room again because the treehouse is so draughty and I figured it didn't make any difference where I slept if he could just show up at school in broad daylight. He was in the corner again and he drifted closer, seeming to get taller as he approached the foot of my bed. He bent over me, arms outstretched as if grasping for me. I couldn't see his face below the brim of his hat but I felt his weight pressing down on me. His hands locked around my neck and they were freezing cold, like ice.

I tried to scream but he choked me and I couldn't make a sound or move any part of my body just like before, only this time I couldn't breathe. He squeezed harder and harder as I looked into the black void of his face and saw absolutely nothing.

Then I woke up, gasping for air. I looked at the clock. It was 2:37. My neck still felt cold but I could breathe at least. It took me a long time to go back to sleep because I couldn't stop crying.

When I went into the bathroom this morning to brush my teeth, I saw a purplish bruise around my neck. I examined it closer and there is no mistaking the outline of several long fingers. I wore a scarf today. I don't care if people think I'm weird for wearing one in May. I don't want anybody to see my bruises because I can't explain them.

Whatever he is, I think he's getting stronger. He isn't just shadows anymore. He has a physical strength and I'm scared for my life.

Casey

May 15, 1999

Dear Diary,

Footsteps again, and this time they followed me home. I was babysitting the Nielson kid two streets away. It's been a while since I babysat for them and I thought they might have found somebody else they preferred but they said they had just been so busy with work that they hadn't been going out as much as they used to.

I was worried I might get a visit from Him while I was babysitting. Being home alone is not what I need right now. Well, not home alone exactly, but little Johnny Nielson wouldn't exactly be much help, so you know what I mean.

The evening went fine and I had no creepy experiences. It wasn't a late one anyway and the Nielsons were home by ten. I did some studying and then checked my emails on their family computer as well as goofed around on ICQ a little.

I left just after ten and walked home like I usually do after babysitting for them. Mr. Nielson has stopped offering me a ride after I insisted on walking the first few times but I really could have used one tonight but felt too silly asking. So, I walked.

I was heading down our drive when I started hearing the footsteps. It was dark and there was nobody else about, but I could hear a man's footsteps some distance behind me. Every time I stopped, the footsteps stopped too, a little after mine. Almost like an echo.

I kept turning around to see if I was being followed and every time I did, I thought I could see some tall figure in the shade of the bushes or behind a parked car, always just beyond the reach of the streetlights. I would continue walking and the footsteps would start again, matching me pace for pace.

The last time I turned around, I was sure that somebody was standing there watching me because the shadow was very still against the movement of the wind in the trees. It looked so much like the outline of a tall man in a brimmed hat.

I turned around and quickened my pace. The footsteps quickened too and, my heart feeling like it was going to burst, I broke into a run as I approached my house. I could hear the footsteps running too, trying to catch me! I ran up our path and into the house, slamming the door behind me without looking back. I glanced through the peephole, terrified that I might see an eye staring back at me but there was nothing there. No shadows up and down the street for as far as I could see. I didn't dare open the door.

It's 10:45 now and I can't escape the feeling that I've just had a very close call. The bruise on my neck is still there but is starting to fade. I hope He doesn't visit me again tonight.

I have a theory. Whatever these delusions or – God forbid – visitations are, they seem to be connected with my use of the internet or computers in general. Every time I see the Hat Man, it always happens just after I've been online. Everything was fine at the Nielson's until I used their computer and then got chased home by the Hat Man. And those creepy glitches where it feels like somebody is copying my actions online? It's kind of like an online shadow. Only a bad shadow that wants to mess with me, just like the Hat Man. Is that Him online, twisting my words and pretending he's me?

I feel like I'm going mad, not knowing who to trust or what is even real. Only you, dear Diary, are real. You are the only thing I can trust. One thing is for sure. I can't trust computers or the internet. It's all lies. A big black window of lies.

Casey

May 16, 1999

I don't dare go online and I keep my PC turned off. No dreams last night and nothing today. Things are almost back to normal. But I need to find out what this thing is.

I wish I could talk to Riley, but she just seems so uncommunicative lately. I don't know what I've done to annoy her. She's good with computers and would be able to figure out if mine has some sort of a virus. Maybe it's the weird stuff that happens to me online that messes with my head and makes me see things. But I feel like she won't believe me, like she didn't with the webcam thing.

The only other person I can think of who might be able to help is Chloe, my old friend from grade school. Remember her? We haven't spoken since that awful day in eighth grade after gym class. We just move in different circles now. She's a goth and I just don't know how to talk to her anymore. But nobody in school is more of a wizard with computers. Seriously, she is always in the lab doing stuff on the net I don't even understand. All the teachers go to her for help so why shouldn't I? I just don't know how to approach her after all these years and ask her for a favor.

Why is this so hard?

Casey

May 17, 1999

I saw Chloe in the hallway today. I so wanted to talk to her, but I just couldn't. How is it possible we have drifted so far apart?

You, my dearest Diary, are the only proof I dare record. I don't want to write anything on my computer because I feel sure the Hat Man will read it. That's where he is, inside the computer. I don't even want to turn it on. I know it sounds crazy but I'm sure of it. I will keep on recording everything that happens in these pages. Every night I hide you in the treehouse. My dad helped Chloe and I build it in fifth grade and it feels like an appropriate hiding spot. We were so happy in those days, and I know that if anything happens to me, she'll find you and learn the truth.

Chloe, if you are reading this, I am sorry for what happened between us. I wish we were still friends. But, if you are reading this, then I guess I'm dead. I don't understand what is happening to me but maybe you will. Be careful, Chloe. There is something in the internet and it is evil.

I love you and miss you,

Casey

May 20, 1999

Dear Diary,

Things are much better. Since I've stopped going online and have kept my PC turned off, I have had no more bad dreams or waking terrors. The Hat Man has left me alone and I am sure now that it was all something to do with my use of the internet. Maybe I was overworking myself, stressing about my finals and then spending so many nights writing that stupid story. I might have had some sort of psychotic break. God, it feels scary to write that. I guess I should seek help in case it happens again but I really don't want anybody to know how crazy I am. They might lock me away. Just don't tell anyone, Diary! This is between us, OK?

Tonight is going to be the big test. Riley is being a lot more friendly and keeps bugging me about never being online lately. Apparently, I'm missing lots of afterschool gossip about Freddie's online GF! I've been missing them all too and I miss our late night chats on ICQ but I've just been so scared to use the computer after all that's happened. So, tonight, I'm going to join them online and prove to myself that all the nightmares are over once and for all. This is part of my healing process. If I can go the evening using the net like normal, then I will know that I am finally free of the Hat Man.

Wish me luck!

Love, Casey

The preceding was Casey's last entry. She was found dead later that night.

Beauty in Darkness: The Online Journal of Chloe Evans (06/07/99)

June 07, 1999

I finished reading Casey's diary and I'm crying so much, even as I write this. She tried to call out to me. In her darkest days before her death, she tried to reach me, but I was deaf to her pleas. I feel so fucking awful for not being there for her. For not being her friend at the last.

I need to get this diary to the police but also, I need to make sure Casey's parents are in the loop. I have no idea how I'm going to explain it all to them and part of me thinks they'd be better off not reading the damn thing, but they have to. And the police? I don't know what they can deduce from it all other than that Casey was crazy.

But was she? I don't even know anymore. Her diary is just too wild and creepy to be believed. But with what happened to Freddie and Phil and then what Riley told me? It can't just be a coincidence. Riley was right about one thing; it is all connected. It has to be. I just don't know how.

I feel like I should tell you what I read in the pages of Casey's diary, but it wouldn't be right to post her private thoughts on the net for all to see. I made a copy of the diary (which took me about an hour down at the local library) so if there is any truth to Riley's concerns about a conspiracy, I, at least, will have a copy of Casey's last words. I'm debating how much of it I should share with you. Maybe some. Maybe none. But for now, let's just say that Casey felt like she was being stalked by something that emanated from the net itself. Some shadowy figure in a black hat who appeared in the corner of her room at night. She even thinks she saw him in her webcam feed.

I have no doubt that this shadow man was what pursued her to her death that night, causing her to die of a heart attack. He literally scared her to death. But was he the same thing Phil was seeing before he died? Did this mysterious 'hat man' make him carve up his own face? And what of Freddie? Riley was convinced that somebody was threatening him online. Mr. Hat Man again? I wish I knew.

I feel I have learned all I can from Casey's diary and I'm not much closer to uncovering the truth. I need to follow my next lead. I've been thinking about this a lot. If there really is something dangerous in the net, then surely others have also been affected? I want to contact this mysterious Motix21 Riley was in contact with before all this bad stuff happened. He's apparently some great hacker and was deep into this game-that-Riley-thinks-isn't-a-game. I need to track him down and find out what he knows.

Looks like I'll be spending my evening on Usenet and IRC, not that I don't spend most of my evenings on there already.

I'll keep you updated, my gothlings.

Stay dark and beautiful \m/

INCIDENT REPORT FROM SPRING GROVE HOSPITAL CENTER (06/07/99)

DATE OF INCIDENT: 06/06/99

DATE OF REPORT: 06/07/99

REPORTING PHYSICIAN: Dr. Andrew Scully

PATIENT: Riley Parker

Details of Incident: Nurses alerted me at 11:31 p.m. of a disturbance in the patient's room. Noises had been heard and the patient appeared to be gravely injured. When I came to the patient's room, I found her lying on the floor, on her left side, in a pool of blood. Her head had suffered severe trauma from repeated and violent contact with the wall. The nurse kneeling at her side, was attempting to render aid but it was too late. I pronounced the patient's time of death at 11:37 p.m.

Treatment: None possible

Commentary: The trauma to the patient's head appears to be self-inflicted. The patient's mental state had deteriorated in the past two days and the patient's death is therefore, in my opinion, suicide.

BEAUTY IN DARKNESS: THE ONLINE JOURNAL OF CHLOE EVANS (06/08/99 – 06/12/99)

June 8, 1999

This Motix guy seems to be something of a legend. I guess I've just been out of the game for a while, otherwise I would have heard of him. I hit up a few hackers I used to shoot the shit with on Usenet and they'd all heard of him to varying degrees. One guy, Hooternanny66 (who had been my associate on the great UCLA hack of '97), straight up asked me if I was looking into the disappearance of Crawdaddy2281. That knocked me back a bit because it was the first outside confirmation of what Riley had told me.

"You know about Crawdaddy?" I asked him.

"What you YOU know about Crawdaddy?" he fired back.

We talked for about an hour and he pretty much confirmed everything Riley had told me about the so-called 'game'. He also tried to warn me off the whole thing.

"Seriously, be careful when dealing with these guys."

"Why?"

"Crawdaddy just disappeared off the map because he found out too much. It's no wonder Motix is keeping a low profile."

"Wasn't Crawdaddy arrested?"

"No, I mean like, he totally vanished. There's no trace of him online. People who spoke to him remember him but every conversation he had with anybody is gone. It's like he never existed. You can't find him anywhere. It takes some serious skills to unperson somebody like that on the net."

But Motix is still around?"

"As far as I know. But there are rumors about him too that should make you want to stay clear."

"Such as?"

"That he's a government spy, or a foreign agent. That he knows more about Crawdaddy's disappearance than he's letting on."

"What's that based on?"

"I don't know. They're just rumors. I'm just saying, be careful."

I was up most of the night scouring various newsgroups for more leads. Hooternanny was right about Crawdaddy. There's nothing from him anywhere. The only mentions of his name are from people wondering where he went. He's just ... gone. And as for Motix, I need to keep looking. If he's out there, I need to talk to him.

That's all for now. \m/ Stay dark and beautiful, gothlings.

June 9, 1999

Holy Fuck, Motix just contacted me!

I guess I made enough ripples online that he heard I was looking for him and decided to hit me up! I don't know how he got my ICQ number (I barely use the damn thing and prefer IRC) but I got a message from him around eleven last night. He was pretty cryptic and I guess he wants to test me out before he tells me too much about himself. I copy-pasted our brief conversation below;

Motix21 – Hello.

BeautyInDarkness – Uhhhh, Hi?

Motix21 – You have been looking for me.

BeautyInDarkness – Yeah. But you found me. This is THE Motix21, right?

Motix21 – In the flesh.

BeautyInDarkness – You were in contact with a friend of mine. Riley Parker?

Motix21 - ?

BeautyInDarkness – I think she went by Princess something. Some anime name.

Motix21 – PrincessKirigoe?

BeautyInDarkness – Yeah. Sounds like her.

Motix21 – How is she?

BeautyInDarkness – Not good. They've got her locked up in a mental institute. She got pretty freaked out by whatever you guys were getting into.

Motix21 – That's too bad. First Crawdaddy. Then PrincessKirigoe. There have been many others.

BeautyInDarkness – Others? How many? And what happened to them?

Motix21 – Are you sure you want to know? Haven't there been warnings enough?

BeautyInDarkness – I want to know. I NEED to know. Kids at my school are dropping like flies ...

Motix21 – Then it is spreading.

BeautyInDarkness – What is spreading?

Motix21 – Just know that once you start down this path, there will be no turning back. It is too late for me. But you might ...

BeautyInDarkness – I can take it. I have to stop more people I know dying. Tell me!

Motix21 - http://sapphiraindex.com

BeautyInDarkness – Huh? What's that?

Motix21 – You tell me.

BeautyInDarkness – It's ... a website. Just a black screen with a login bar. What's the password?

Motix21 – Nobody knows. Before he disappeared, Crawdaddy uploaded several binary files to Usenet. They were massive. The files were hosted by this site.

BeautyInDarkness – Sooooo, the site belongs to Crawdaddy?

Motix21 – Not necessarily. He may have cracked the password and uploaded the files. Then somebody got to him. The files were the last things he communicated.

BeautyInDarkness – Has anybody been able to decrypt the files?

Motix21 – No. They were incomplete. Crawdaddy was unable to finish the job. This website is the key. Crack the site, find the answers. Goodbye for now.

BeautyInDarkness – Wait, you're going? I still have so many questions!

Motix21 – I'm not sure I have the answers. But keep looking. Maybe together we can find them.

He logged off after that, leaving me super frustrated but not without an avenue for my frustrations. This site. It's weird. After examining the frontend JavaScript, I can see that the site has an embedded media player. There's a LOT of open ports, meaning that the server is most likely used for file hosting and sharing. The binary files that Crawdaddy was trying to smuggle out of the server are undoubtedly media files, but of what nature?

I feel kinda nervous fooling around with something like this after all that Riley has told me. Way too many theories are running through my head. Could this site be linked to the JPL or some other government affiliated department? I don't want to bite off more than I can chew and piss off the wrong people but there is a mystery here and I haven't done anything illegal. I'm going to pursue this, no matter where it leads.

I looked up who registered the domain. When somebody sets up a site, they are required to register their name as a matter of public record. That means you can look up whoever owns a particular domain. The Sapphira Index was set up in 1997 by an Austin Carola. I did a reverse domain name search to see if he had registered any other websites. Austin Carola isn't an extremely uncommon name so the DNS came up with four or five websites, but there was only one under the same domain registrar as the Sapphira Index. It was founded the same year the Sapphira Index was and when I visited the site, I came across a fairly amateurish page for a web cafe in Southern California.

Tomorrow, I'm going to hit up some usual suspects on Usenet and ask if anybody lives near the address provided on the website and if they can check it out for me. Right now, I need some sleep, but I don't know if I'm going to get any. This whole thing is bugging me out and I want answers.

\m/ Goodnight, gothlings. Stay dark and beautiful.

Didn't sleep much. My computer was calling to me like a siren all through the night. My brain wouldn't let me rest. It wanted to pursue the mystery. I resisted my impulses until around seven, before calling the school to say that I was sick. Then I smoked a clove and took a valium before hitting the newsgroups. I put out the address of the web cafe and explained that it was part of the whole Crawdaddy mystery but held back on the Sapphira Index website and what Motix had told me. Stuff like this is like catnip for all the conspiracy theorists out there and this whole thing could rapidly get out of hand. I feel safe telling you, dear gothlings, because the Usenet guys are a whole different crowd. They barely use the web.

Lo and behold, my old buddy Hooternanny told me that he lives in Southern California and would be happy to check out the address. This is breaking new ground. We hackers NEVER give out personal info, not even what state we live in, even to each other. Hooternanny must be pretty keen to help me to let himself slip like that. He's off work at four and will check out the address.

Anyway, Motix hit me up again this afternoon and was much more talkative. We had a seriously long discussion and not just about the Crawdaddy thing. It got personal and he revealed himself to be a pretty awesome guy. We shot the shit about stuff (and, yes, I was careful not to make Hooternanny's mistake by giving away anything personal). Mostly generic shit about hacking, movies and music. Here's a little snippet which shows what a cool guy he is.

Motix21 – So, you seem to be a pretty accomplished hacker.

BeautyInDarkness – You mean for a girl, right?

Motix21 – Not at all. That's completely irrelevant. I'm just impressed with what you've told me so far.

BeautyInDarkness – Sorry. Don't mean to be so defensive. But people always think that just because I'm a girl, then I'm just some dumb script kiddie.

Motix21 – I hate that gatekeeping bullshit. I know you're an accomplished hacker, but even if you weren't, so what? What's the point of deriding a person with a stupid world like that? It's only so they can feel big about themselves. It's like when goths get all high and mighty about Marilyn Manson fans or people who wear striped stockings, calling them 'mall goths' and not 'real goths'. It's the same bullshit as 'script kiddies'.

BeautyInDarkness – Haha! Yeah, I've been called a mall goth almost as many times as I've been called a script kiddie. It used to bother me, but I don't give a fuck anymore. Let them think what they want to.

Motix21 – That's the spirit ;-p

We seem to be kindred spirits. His favorite movie is also *The Crow* and he likes NIN and Korn. I know I need to be careful, but I can't help wondering where he lives and if it's anywhere near me. Damn, I need a date!

Shit. While I was writing this, I got a message from Hooternanny. He checked out the address! Says it's a vacant lot and looks like it's been vacant for years, all grown over with weeds and stuff. What the hell? This domain was registered two years ago, and no web café was built? Hooternanny still wants to know more about what this address is and how it's connected to Crawdaddy. I don't know if I should tell him. I mean, I trust him enough after that whole UCLA hack, but I don't want to drag more people into this than strictly necessary.

I'm going to continue trying to find out as much as I can about this elusive Austin Carola but I think I'm going to focus most of my efforts on cracking the password on the Sapphira Index site. It's going to be a challenge and I'm a little rusty but I think I'm up to it.

\m/ Stay dark and beautiful, gothlings.

June 11, 1999

Bad news when I got to school today. Everybody found out yesterday, but I was playing hooky, so I didn't get the message. Riley died a few days ago. The word is that it was suicide. She was the last of that group of friends. They're all dead now. Will that be an end to it? Not if I've got anything to say about it. Riley's death is just more fuel to my fire. I *will* find out what killed them!

Dug up some info on Austin Carola and it's not good. First I emailed the address on his internet café site. While I waited for an answer I figured wouldn't come, I called the office of the County Clerk-Recorder and asked about the property deed information for the vacant lot. They told me I had to send a written request by mail or fax (or turn up in person). I went down to the library and faxed a request and gave my email address. A few hours later, I received an email confirming that Austin Carola does indeed own the lot.

I looked up the company information for Mr. Carola's internet café and found that paperwork for an LLC was filed in 1997 by Austin Carola who was his own registered agent with an address in San Francisco. The address of the vacant lot was given as the business address. I did a little digging into the website of California's Secretary of State office (which is laughably easy to hack, by the way) and found a few emails that were sent back and forth between the office and Mr. Carola. There was nothing in them that suggested anything strange.

So far, so vanilla. Everything about the vacant lot and the internet café checks out. Except one thing.

Austin Carola is dead.

While I was waiting for answers from various offices, I looked for anything I could find online about Mr. Carola of Southern California. There wasn't much so I resorted to the old Yellow Pages. There was a number for 'Carola, Austin & Sandy' with an address in San Francisco. I called it and a woman answered.

Now, how the hell do I explain who I am and why I'm calling? I somehow muddled through, sticking as close to the truth as possible. I told her I was interested in the vacant lot Mr. Carola owns. She knew nothing about that and told me that her brother had died some years ago.

"Years ago?" I asked, after offering my condolences.

"November of 1996," Sandy Carola replied.

That makes no sense. How could a dead man register a company, purchase a lot and set up a domain a year after his death?

"May I ask how he died?" I said, tentatively, expecting her to slam the phone down on me.

There was a long pause. "Do you know something about my brother's death?" she asked.

"Uh, no, not at all," I admitted. "I just find it weird that there is a vacant lot in his name."

"That is weird," she said. "But weird is something I've just gotten used to."

"How so?"

"Well, Austin was a secretive guy. I don't really know how he died. The coroner called it a heart attack and the cops thought it was drugs but Austin wasn't like that. He was a bit of a computer nerd but in the weeks before his death he just got so obsessed with that damned thing. He wasn't eating or sleeping much and then, one day. He disappeared."

"Disappeared?"

"He was gone for a week. I was worried sick and the cops were next to useless. Eventually somebody found his body in an abandoned warehouse. He must have suffered a psychotic break or something and just wandered in there to die of heart failure."

Heart failure. Just like Casey.

"He never expressed any interest in setting up an internet café?" I asked.

"No. What an odd question!"

"Never mind. Was he acting strange before he ... disappeared?" I asked.

"Yeah. He was spending a hell of a lot of time online, and I never figured out what he was looking at. His internet history was scrubbed before he left."

"Was he ever threatened by anybody?"

"Like who?"

"I don't know, did he show any signs of paranoia, like he was being followed?"

"Not really. You sound an awful lot like the police. What did you say your name was again?"

I hung up on her after mumbling some apologies for disturbing her. I guess I could have told her all about the kids at my school and how it might all be connected to her brother and his weirdo website. But what good would that do? I have no answers to console her with. Maybe, once I've figured all this out, I'll call her again and come clean.

But in the meantime, I have a website to crack. Austin Carola was a literal dead end, so all I have left is the mysterious site somebody set up under his name. The more I look into this, the weirder it gets. I'm going to go make a big pot of coffee and then I'm going to knuckle down and get hacking.

Wish me luck, gothlings \m/ Stay dark and beautiful.

June 12, 1999

I did it.

It took nearly all night, but I fucking did it. I hacked the Sapphira Index. I gave up on brute force methods with one of my own password generator tools and started trying SQL injections. Around three this morning, I finally gained access.

And HOLY SHIT.

The site is linked to an encrypted server folder containing hundreds of terabytes worth of files. I mean fucking HUNDREDS. That's ridiculous. Nothing on the net has that much data storage. What the hell is all this stuff? My worries about a secret government site were instantly pushed aside by more insidious theories. What could take up this much space? A whole library of pirated movies? Child porn? Snuff films?

I was right about the media player. I can access the files directly from the website and view them. There are all sorts of file types here and none of it is organized into subfolders. I randomly checked out a couple and they really were random, like *randomly mundane* but their existence behind this mysterious security wall renders them ... unsettling in their mundanity.

The first one was just a security cam feed of some parking lot somewhere. I watched a couple of vehicles come and go but there was nothing of note. The next one was from somebody's web cam. I sat and watched some Asian guy's face for about fifteen minutes while he dicked around on his computer, expecting something – *anything* – to happen, but nothing did. If this is the kind of shit hidden away in the Sapphira Index, then no wonder it's taking up hundreds of terabytes. I just can't figure out why anybody wants to collect this stuff. The thought of *how* they collected it gives me the heebie-jeebies.

It occurred to me to search for anything related to Casey and the others. If this weird-ass site really is connected to whatever Riley got involved in, then perhaps there'll be some files on them. Sure enough, I found four text files with their names in the titles. I opened Casey's first. Read it, then moved on to Freddies, and Phil's and Riley's. They're all there. And now I know what connects them all. Now I know what connects them to the Sapphira Index.

In Casey's diary, she mentioned that they had all submitted short horror stories to an online competition offering a cash prize. I never thought about whatever became of that contest because, well, their deaths kind of made it irrelevant. BUT THEIR STORIES ARE FUCKING HERE! Right here in the Sapphira Index! I don't know how they got here or if that online contest was part of the whole thing but there is something about the stories themselves which sent a shiver through me.

I really can't explain it to you. It's just too weird and too hard to pin down, but there is something just *off* about those stories, like they are predicting something. I feel I have no way of conveying this to you without posting the stories here for you to read for yourselves. So ... that's what I'm doing. Here they are; four stories written by   the   dead.

A Place of Hurt (Casey's Story)

I was bored. It was a Saturday night, and I had no plans. None of my friends were doing anything interesting and they weren't online. I did what I usually do when I have nothing to do with my time and surfed the web, clicking from site to site on different webrings, usually of the true crime or unexplained phenomena variety. I love that stuff. Ghosts, serial killers, cryptozoology, aliens. I know most of the stuff online is B.S. but it's still fun to peruse people's crazy sites which do such a good job of making it seem real. There's something about the internet which feels much more real and dangerous than TV or magazines. I guess it's because everybody's anonymous and you never know if what you are reading is real or not.

That was how I stumbled upon a site called 'A Place of Hurt'.

It was a simple Geocities site with a black background and a series of pages laid out like an online journal. There was no sitemap or menu. Only two arrows with which to navigate the journal entries.

The first one was dated only a month ago and I realized I had stumbled over a nearly brand-new site. I read the first entry.

21 February 1999

I have been watching her for a week now.

Soon, my darling. Soon.

There was a black and white picture accompanying the entry. It showed a young woman, about my age, walking down a crowded high street. There were plenty of other people on the street, but it was clear that she was the focus of the photograph. Her head was turned to one side and her dark, wavy hair was swept to one side to reveal a pretty face. She didn't seem to know that she was being photographed. Just a random teenager going about her business but photographed from afar.

Well, this was weird. It seemed like the author of the site was stalking this girl. For real? Maybe. It was just too vague and non-eventful to be a work of fiction. But there were more entries to follow, and I clicked on the arrow at the bottom of the page.

23 February 1999

I think she saw me this time. I need to make my move soon. I can't wait any longer. I don't WANT to wait any longer. Soon, you will be mine, my darling.

Two pictures accompanied the post this time, and the first one caused a shiver to ripple down my spine. It was of the same girl, only she was in bed this time, asleep. The picture seemed to have been taken through the slats of a closet or something as black bars obscured much of the image. The girl's face was visible in a band of light from an open door that led to the landing beyond.

The next picture was almost identical. The same black bars cut across the image showing that the photographer was still inside the closet only this time the girl wasn't asleep. She was sitting up in bed, looking in the direction of the photographer, her eyes wide and terrified, staring directly at the camera.

I think she saw me this time.

If she did then she hadn't had the courage to investigate the closet. If this was real, then it was just about the creepiest thing I had ever found on the net. I clicked 'next', my heart trembling at what might be on the next page.

I skipped the text and scrolled down to the images. There were four this time and I almost felt relieved when I saw them for they all but confirmed that what I was reading was fake. The girl was the subject in all four images (which took their sweet time in loading), and she appeared to be dead. Two of the pictures were closeups of her face and the other two were taken several feet away showing her naked body, artfully positioned so her nipples and pubic region could not be seen. She was lying in some grassy ditch someplace where the sunlight shining through the trees made shadows of the branches on her pale skin. Her throat looked like it had been cut and blood covered her bare breasts. She looked like a plastic doll somebody had mocked up for Halloween.

Well, that confirmed it. The site was a fake. It had to be. There was simply no way a murderer would post pictures of his victim along with text that was as good as a confession. I read the entry.

27 February 1999

It is done. She struggled a bit (they always do) but my knife showed her who is boss. I got very messy and had to burn my clothes. They'll never find me.

It was the last entry, strengthening my conviction that none of it was real. It was just a dumb prank. The sick lengths some people went to in order to trick people online! But I had to admit, it had me going for a while and I had got a kick out of it. *Mission accomplished, whoever you are,* I thought as I switched off my PC and got ready for bed.

I had nearly forgotten about 'A Place of Hurt' until the following week when something happened which dragged it back into the forefront of my mind. I had just got home from cheerleading practice and my dad had the evening news on in the living room.

"... a huge operation to find the missing nineteen-year-old, but today her family received the tragic news that a body found in the woods nearby her home has been positively identified as that of Lindsey Hamilton. The condition of the body suggests that she had been there for nearly a month."

A photo of the deceased flashed up on the TV screen and my heart skipped a beat. Nausea choked me and my knees started to buckle as I grasped the kitchen counter for support. The photo of the dead girl was the same girl I had seen on that weird website. There was no mistaking it.

"Lindsey Hamilton, described by classmates as kind and sensitive, vanished on her way home over a month ago," the anchorwoman went on. "Police detectives say that she was murdered at an unknown location and her body dumped in the woods. The hunt for her killer goes on."

"Awful thing," my dad said as the anchorwoman turned to the next topic. "Not too far from here, either."

"Where?" I asked breathlessly.

"Baltimore."

I swallowed. That was too close for comfort, but I had something worse on my mind than geographical distance. I had read the killer's confession!

There was no sitting on this. I told my parents all about what I had read and tried to show them the website, but when I eventually found it in my browser history and clicked on it, all I got was a '404 page not found' screen. The site had been removed.

There was a perfectly good explanation for this. If the killer had any kind of smarts, he would have removed his confession when the body of Lindsey Hamilton had been discovered. But, as it was only just appearing on the news, how quickly had he acted?

My parents were infuriatingly blasé about it all and didn't seem to believe me. They tried to make out like I was mistaken, that I had seen a picture of somebody who *looked* like Lindsey Hamilton.

My mom actually said; "There are a lot of sick jokes on the net. Not everything you read online is real, you know?"

I could have screamed.

It *was* real, I knew that now and the killer was trying to cover up his tracks. I had peeked inside the mind of a murderer, and I knew I couldn't let it rest. I had to find out more about 'A Place of Hurt'. If he had posted online about his crimes, then he might do it again. Isn't that what they say about serial killers? That they have a pathological need to revisit the site of their crimes or toy with the police, almost like they want to get caught.

I spent several evenings scanning webrings and asking questions in chatrooms, trying to see if anybody knew anything about the site. After all, if I had stumbled across it, somebody else must have. Eventually, somebody answered my prayers.

MidniteMan33 > *Is this what you're looking for? [Hyperlink].*

I hurriedly clicked on the link they provided and was brought to what looked like an exact copy of 'A Place of Hurt' right down to the font and layout. There was only one entry, brutally short, dated a day ago.

19 March 1999

I have a new toy.

The image below the text showed a different girl walking in a park, clutching a stack of schoolbooks to her chest. Once again, she was about my age, pretty and, by the look of her, a little shy and mild-mannered.

I wanted to scream out to her, reach through the computer screen and warn her that she had drawn the attention of a serial killer. There had to be something I could do. I would not sit by and watch this monster stalk and slay her as he had done to Lindsey Hamilton.

I put on my detective hat and tried to do what I could to prevent the awfulness that was gathering over this oblivious girl's head like a thundercloud. I bookmarked the page, took a screengrab and downloaded the image of the girl. I would share it all over the web forums and try to find her before she too was brutally murdered.

I posted the link to 'A Place of Hurt' and asked if anybody in the Baltimore area recognized the girl or the park. Nobody seemed particularly interested as the site had nothing on it but the picture and the hauntingly cryptic entry which meant nothing to anybody except me and the killer. I resorted to scare tactics, saying that this was a matter of life and death and that the girl in the picture was in grave danger. Pretty much everybody brushed me off as a jokester and replied to my pleas for help with laughing emoticons. Then one poster gave me a lifeline.

SnarlyWWW > *It looks like Patterson Park in Baltimore but I can't be sure.*

It wasn't much, but it was something. I decided to go to the police without telling my mom and dad. They'd only try to convince me I was overreacting again.

The police weren't much better. I told the officer at the desk about the website and, after a while trying to bring it up on his computer without luck, he gave me the email address of a Detective Biderman and told me to send the link to him. I did so as soon as I got home but didn't hear anything. I figured that I was put down as just another crazy kid or somebody trying a hoax.

The next day, 'A Place of Hurt' was updated.

22 March 1999

Peekaboo! I see you!

The accompanying image showed a grainy, low-quality image of the same girl's face very close up and at first, I thought it was a shot of her dead body. Then I realized that her eyes were open and she was looking down, as if at a keyboard, almost a mirror of myself as I gazed into my PC monitor. This was taken from a webcam!

I could see the girl's bedroom wall behind her and could make out a poster of The Backstreet Boys. The killer was watching her from her own computer! The thought was so nauseatingly creepy that I thanked God that I didn't have a webcam. How could he hack her computer like that? But if it was connected to the internet, I guessed it was possible.

Creepy as it was, it was more evidence, and I sent a second email to Detective Biderman with a link to the updated site. "You HAVE to do something!" I wrote. "This girl is in DANGER!"

Once again, I got no reply from the detective, and I wondered if he was even getting my emails or if they were going directly into a slush folder. Another day passed and I was in agony, knowing that the killer was closing in on that poor girl and there was nothing I could do about it.

24 March 1999

I especially enjoyed this one! She was a real wriggler!

I felt sick as I read the words, knowing that I was too late. The killer had struck again, and that sweet, innocent girl was dead.

Thankfully, no image accompanied the text but there was an embedded RealPlayer video. My gut churned as my cursor hovered over it. Did I really want to see it? Surely it would be better to leave it to the police?

But the police weren't interested. I was completely alone in this, and I knew I had to watch the video. At the very least, it might provide another clue in identifying the killer. He might get careless and reveal something about himself or his location. With a trembling hand, I clicked 'play'.

It took around twenty minutes to buffer and I paced my bedroom, unable to leave the vicinity of my PC for too long. I *had* to see what was on that video, even though I was terrified of *what* I might actually see.

Eventually, after a torturously long wait, the video was ready for me to watch. I sat down, my heart thudding and a cold sweat on my forehead as the clip started.

I saw the girl. She was crying. Her glasses were gone and she was stripped down to her underwear. She seemed to be strapped to a surgical-looking table. I tried to make out the surroundings but the image quality was so low and the surroundings so dark that I couldn't make anything out.

Then I saw the contraption at the end of the table, just above the girl's head.

If you've ever seen a bacon slicer in a butcher's shop, you'll have a good idea of what I mean. This was a large one on an industrial scale. I couldn't see if the blade was rotating, but the light glinted off its razor-sharp edge.

The girl suddenly started struggling as she grew even more terrified by something. The video didn't appear to have any sound and I wondered what had happened in that dingy room to make her break out in a sudden panic.

Then I realized I had the volume turned down on my speakers. I reached out and turned it up, just a little, and my ears were filled with the frantic wailing of the girl, rendered tinny by the low-quality RealTime audio.

There was a low humming along with the girl's screams and I knew then that the bacon slicer was running. I noticed too, that it appeared to be on thin rails that ran down the length of the surgical table on either sides of the girl's head. As I watched, it started to move slowly, along the rails, powered by a hidden motor.

I swallowed in a dry throat as it dawned on me what was about to happen. Unable to look away, but dearly wishing I could, I watched as the gleaming circular blade crept closer and closer to the top of the girl's head.

She writhed in her bonds and jerked spasmodically, screaming all the while as the blade drifted closer and closer. Her screams mutated into an agonized wail as the blade sheared through the top layer of skin and hair, scalping her and letting the ugly, disc-shaped slice of flesh and hair follicles tumble to one side.

I forced down nausea as the blade continued its path through the girl's skull, one thin slice at a time. She continued screaming as it worked down her forehead, her arms and legs jerking in their straps, her gradually diminishing brain still conscious, still feeling the pain as it was sliced into 1/8" slivers. On the other side of the reddened blade, perfectly round circles of brain surrounded by white rings of bone and flesh leaned neatly against each other like delicacies in a butcher's window.

Please make it stop ... I prayed. *Please God let this be a nightmare and let me wake up!*

The girl's thrashings subsided as the circular blade reached her eyebrows. Her wide and pain-wracked eyes continued staring straight ahead while the blade continued. Surely, she must be dead by now? Her brain was stacked up like salami. The twitching in her limbs must be nerves giving their last, frantic signals.

As the blade reached her eyeballs, the white jelly of them was ripped apart and spattered the machinery and then the video clip stopped.

That was it. That was the end. I had seen it all and it had been the very worst thing I could have imagined. It would haunt me for the rest of my life, and I was no closer to finding out anything about this monster who butchered young women.

The nausea I had been holding back for so long boiled up in my throat and I leaned down, grasping for the wastepaper basket to hurl the contents of my stomach into.

I never looked at 'A Place of Hurt' again. I refused to. Why subject myself to the amusements of a sick psychopath when there was nothing I could do about it and nobody believed me in any case? I could just spare myself the horrors of it all by throwing in the towel and pretending I had never seen it. Other girls might be abducted and murdered, sure, but what could I do about it? I had tried but if the police weren't going to get involved, then what possible chance did I have of saving them?

But the police did get involved. At last. It was two days after I had watched the sick video of that girl getting murdered that I received a call from the detective I had been pestering with links to 'A Place of Hurt'. He asked me to come down to the station with my parents to make a formal statement.

My parents were confused and a little pissed that I had struck up a conversation with the cops without going through them but, considering that I had gone to them first and they hadn't believed me, I think they felt guilty enough not to kick up too much of a fuss.

They drove me down to the station and we sat in an interview room while Detective Biderman grilled me about the website link and screengrab I had sent him. The link led to a 404 page as the killer had promptly deleted his site again, but it was the image that had the detective interested.

"And you say you don't know this girl at all?" he asked me.

"No," I replied. "As I told you, I found the image on the website."

"A website which no longer exits."

"Because the killer deleted it after he murdered that girl!" I replied, letting my anger get the better of me. "And I saw it happen! I saw that girl's brain get sliced into ribbons and it could have been prevented if you had just listened to me in the first place!"

"Calm down, young lady," said Detective Biderman. "I'm just trying to piece all this together. You say you saw a video clip of this girl being murdered? Specifically that her, *ahem*, 'brain got sliced'?"

"Look, detective, is my daughter charged with anything?" my dad asked, losing his own cool a little. "She's tried to help you as best she can ..."

"Sir," said the detective, "Please understand my interest in your daughter's foreknowledge of this murder. It makes her a valuable asset in this case."

"Foreknowledge of this murder?" my dad repeated. "Are you saying this isn't just some sick online prank?"

"No, sir. The girl in the image your daughter emailed to me was found dead yesterday in a wooded area just outside Baltimore. The top part of her head was missing. Cut cleanly off, just above the eyes."

That shut my dad up. My mom started crying and, after some more questions, we were finally allowed to go home.

I refused to do any more. I wasn't going to look for 'A Place of Hurt' again. I had done my detective bit and had seen far more than I had ever wanted to. It was in the hands of the police now. Let them deal with it. As far as I was concerned, it was over.

But I knew I had been mentally scarred by what I had seen and, as the days passed, I found it impossible to settle back into normal life. I kept feeling like I was being watched. I grew frightened of being alone, always fearful of the shadows. Even when I was in public, I couldn't escape the sensation that I was being watched, *followed.* I would think I saw somebody in my peripheral vision, only to look around and find that nobody was there. The paranoia was suffocating.

And then I received the email.

The subject field was blank, and it was from an address I didn't recognize but at once made me feel uneasy.

From: midniteman33@agol.com

I have a new toy. What do you think, Laura? Are you ready to watch me play with this one?

I felt frozen with terror. Every new thing I noticed about the email scared me more than the last. It was from *him*, the killer. He knew my name. There was a file attached. And I knew why his email address had made me feel so uneasy. It was because I recognized that name ...

Back when I had been trying to find 'A Place of Hurt' after it had been deleted the first time, somebody in a chatroom had sent me the link to the killer's new site. Their name had been MidniteMan33.

I fought back tears as I bitterly reproached myself for being so stupid. I had not even considered that I was putting myself in danger with my online detective work. But I had drawn the attention of the killer, and he knew who I was. He may even know that I had gone to the police. Did that mean that I was next? Was this the start of him toying with me, stalking me like he had the others? Perhaps it hadn't been paranoia which had plagued me the past few days. Perhaps I really had caught glimpses of somebody following me and ducking out of sight before I could get a good look at them.

But the attached file ...

My cursor hovered above it. What awfulness did it contain? I could ignore it. I could delete the email and refuse to engage in his sick games. But this was a direct message from the killer to me. A vital clue, perhaps or at least a warning. Another thought crossed my mind as I remembered the webcam video of the most recent victim. The killer had obviously hacked her computer. Had he sent her a file too? Was it a virus that had given him access to her webcam?

I could drive myself mad going around in circles like this. Before I could give it any more thought, my finger double clicked the attachment without me even telling it to. I knew I had to see what was in that file, even if my computer did get infected. *Let's play, you bastard*, I thought defiantly.

The image was a screengrab that looked like it had been taken from a webcam. How many computers had this guy infected? The person was looking intently at their screen, as if watching or reading something, unaware that they were being watched in return. Then I spotted a shadow behind them, just a black smudge due to the poor quality of the webcam, but it definitely looked like a man standing there, just over their shoulder.

I wanted to scream at the person who sat at their computer that they were in danger. It was like some horrible nightmare that just kept repeating itself. This time I desperately wanted to warn the subject of the killer's new fixation because the oblivious person sitting at their computer ... was you.

Dropping Dox (Freddie's Story)

Be careful who you piss off online. That's the moral of my story up front. You can read the following if you want to, or you can keep on surfing. But please, if you take one thing away from what I'm writing here, then it's *be careful who you piss off online.*

I was a regular user of Usenet newsgroups back in the early days and I posted under the name 'StigOsaur'. I largely hung out on alt.tasteless where nothing was taboo, everybody was anonymous and perversion and bad taste were the names of the game. I would regularly join in flame wars with other newsgroups in which we would take them over by 'crapflooding' i.e. posing massive volumes of often offensive, but largely nonsensical posts which swamped on-topic communication.

Now, creating new newsgroups is a massive hassle so most people just 'colonize' one of the hundreds of abandoned groups already in existence and use it for their own purposes. So, it's really a free-for-all on Usenet. Nobody has more of a right to a group than anybody else and it's strictly mob rule. It was all in good fun. Or at least, it was supposed to be.

When I came across DodiesDiary, I just knew I had to have a little fun with him. Dodie was apparently a dog belonging to a user who posted from his pet's point of view in a dog-related newsgroup under the rec* hierarchy. The posts took the form of diary entries as his username suggested like;

>Diarrhea again today. I don't know why my owner can't find a brand of dry food that doesn't play havoc with my digestive system. Park in the afternoon. Ball chasing is fun!

It was hilarious. I was convinced DodiesDiary was some sort of prankster just messing around. It was just too goofy to be real but most people in the group seemed to be oblivious to his irony and actually engaged with him in efforts to be helpful. They'd give him tips on what his 'owner' should be doing, showing no signs of feeling silly conversing with somebody who was pretending to be a dog.

It was too good to be true and so my campaign of terror began.

My initial post was a response to one of his 'diarrhea' posts which seemed to be asking for help on how to get his owner to change the brand of dog food he was giving him. I suggested that he defecate in his owner's bed by way of a wake-up call.

The responses to my suggestion were humorous, mostly by people who took me seriously and chided me for suggesting something so crude and unhelpful. A few called me out for the joker I was. And that's when I decided to bring in the heavy guns. I informed a few users I knew in alt.tasteless and, after checking out DodiesDiary's group, they came up with a few suggestions of their own which far outdid mine in terms of tastelessness.

Pretty soon, DodiesDiary was inundated with literally hundreds of posts from my fellow crapflooders. The posts became ever cruder and more disgusting, graduating from the scatological to the sexual and eventually to topics of mutilation and torture. Honestly, it went beyond what even I can stomach, but leave it to the alt.tasteless crowd to outdo themselves.

And they really did. DodiesDiary and the other original members of the group tried to defend their turf from our invasion to no avail. We thought it was hilarious. DodiesDiary tried to bozo bin us but we even bypassed his kill files so he couldn't escape our assault.

Now, if you are one of the uninitiated in Usenet speak, kill files (or 'bozo binning') refers to the practice of screening out certain topics or people from your newsreader. It's a way of filtering what you see in a newsgroup. Don't want to see posts from Asshole McShitty? Write a file to screen him out. But the trouble is, you don't know who Asshole McShitty really is, so he can easily continue to crapflood you under a new username. And the sheer number of us raiding DodiesDiary's group meant that he had no hope of screening us all.

And then, one day, he was gone. He just stopped posting. A few of the original people in the group called out to him but he didn't answer and eventually the group was abandoned once more as users dropped out and found other places to hang out.

We figured we'd scared him off Usenet and, while we all congratulated ourselves on our petty act of cyber terrorism, I actually felt a little bad about it. I mean, we were only messing with him but even as the whole thing had started to snowball, I had already begun to feel guilty. Even I can take a joke at my own expense if a joke is all it is, but nobody should be hounded off the internet permanently. What if he had taken it all far more seriously than we had intended? What if he had sunk into a deep depression? What if he had killed himself?

I did my best to ignore these thoughts and told myself that he was likely just fine and had successfully thrown us off his scent and was still on Usenet under a new username. I wished him the best of luck and, as the weeks went by, I thought about him less and less.

And then, out of the blue, my world both online and offline was blown wide open. A message appeared on the group from DodiesDiary. It was the first post from him in a week or so. All it said was;

>StigOsaur's real name is xxxx xxxxxx. His email is xxxxxxxx@aol.com and his home address is;

xxxxx xxxxxxx

Derwood, MD xxxxx

All I could do was stare at the post numbly for a minute or two. Then the panic set in. He had 'dropped dox' on me in Usenet speak. This is the practice of revealing a user's personal details on the net and basically making them public knowledge. I had no idea how he had done it. It takes a hacker to find out who the real person behind a username is, but he had done it, and I was in deep shit.

It's unnecessary to say that I had pissed off a lot of people online in my time. Always the wall of anonymity had protected me but now that wall had been whipped aside like it was no more than a curtain, revealing me sitting at my PC like a half-assed Wizard of Oz.

There was nothing I could do about it. My details were out there and I had to just sit there and take whatever my enemies threw at me.

I got a whole bunch of emails calling me every foul name known to humanity. Some went as far as death threats but, after a while, they slowed to a trickle as people moved on and forgot about me. I stopped posting on Usenet, not wanting to draw further attention to myself and it seemed to work but I was horrendously paranoid. I barely went out and sat tight in my house with the doors locked like I was the last man defending a fort. Every time a car drove past my house, I practically freaked out, but, as usual, the online threats were just that. Threats. Nobody seemed about to make good on their words and I began to grow confident that words were all I'd get.

Then the package arrived.

It was a cardboard box, around a cubic foot in size, and it was heavy. It had been left on my doorstep and there were no postage marks meaning that whoever it was from had delivered it personally.

Now, of course I was wary after having been outed online. Worst case scenario, it could have been a bomb, but I didn't think it would be. It could have been a nasty 'present' from somebody I had offended, so I took it out into my back yard, donned rubber gloves and a face mask, and sliced open the tape with a box cutter.

Inside was a black garbage bag fastened with a zip tie. Now I was sure that this was going to be something unpleasant. Given the scatological nature of much of my antics online, I was expecting a literal sack of shit. Using the box cutter, I opened the bag and at once the stench hit me, despite the mask I was wearing.

It wasn't feces. Dark, congealed blood covered some lumpy objects that had a hint of hair on them. Gagging, I stumbled away from the opened package, my stomach churning and threatening to eject my breakfast. But I had to know what this vile mess somebody had sent me was so, cautiously, I peered into the box and, using my gloved hand, moved some of the grisly objects around.

A chill crept over me as I realized that somebody had mailed me a dismembered dog.

I couldn't tell what breed it was. Something small and yappy. There was a plastic wallet in among the gore, seemingly containing a letter. I plucked it out and ran it under the garden hose to clean off the blood. Opening it, I read the typed note.

To xxxx.

You have taken everything from me. Dodie was my life and you soiled and corrupted him with your vileness to such an extent that I had to destroy him. I simply couldn't look at him the same way after the tirade of grotesqueries unleased in his name by you and your associates. I give him to you now (what is left of him). May you suffer as I have suffered at your hands. I no longer need him for I have a new object to focus my energies on. YOU.

Dodie's (former) owner.

The guy was insane. I had half expected a dead animal as soon as I saw the package on my doorstep. It was the kind of thing a disgruntled person might send somebody but to do that to your own dog ...? It was just so unnecessarily demented that he had to have been a crazy person to begin with. After all, who writes from the point of view of his dog anyway?

But his final words chilled me. Could I expect more packages? It occurred to me to call the cops, but I knew that would likely do more harm than good. After all, I didn't exactly want to let them know that I had unleashed a torrent of crapflooding on some guy's newsgroup. I mean, I don't think I broke any laws, but the cops would most likely fail to sympathize with me.

So, I did only two things. I buried Dodie's remains in my back yard, not wanting the garbage collectors to discover a dismembered dog in my trashcan. And I bought a gun. This psycho knew where I lived and if he tried any more shit, then he'd find me ready.

A couple of days later, another package was left on my doorstep. I had just got home from work, so I didn't know how long it had been there. It was smaller this time. Was he sending me dead mice or some shit now? I took it indoors and opened it. It was a videotape.

I had no option but to shove it in the VCR and hit play to see what this demented maniac was up to now. The fuzzy quality suggested a video recorder and, as the lines cleared, I could see a street scene. Cars, buses, people walking. I recognized it as downtown DC where I worked and got an acutely uneasy feeling.

The crowds parted as whoever was holding the camera jostled their way down the street. They focused in on a figure walking a few feet ahead, and as soon as I saw him, I knew it was me. This must have been taken sometime last week as the coat I was wearing was currently at the drycleaners. The cameraman got right up close to me, and I felt the hairs on the back of my neck prick up, as if he was there in my living room, right behind me.

The thought of that maniac following me on my way to work and getting close enough to breathe down my neck without me even knowing it, was terrifying. I didn't know how dangerous this guy was. All I knew was that he was crazy and he was stalking me.

The videotape cut to another scene, a much more crowded one. It was a rock concert of some sort, and the camera was clearly hidden beneath a coat or inside a bag because a black flap of material obscured part of the lens.

Then I recognized the music and the whole scene clicked into place. It was the HFStival at the RFK Stadium I had gone to with my girlfriend Jennie last week. I had tried to get time off from work but they wouldn't let me, so I had faked the flu and we had gone anyway.

Shit.

There we were in the crowd, rocking away on candid camera at the hands of this bastard.

He had taped me faking sick days at the goddamn HFStival. If my employer saw this, then I was fucked.

The tape ran to black and I fast forwarded to the end but there was nothing more. No note had accompanied it and there had been no threatening text on the tape. It was just an ominous, unspoken threat.

I spent the night worrying about his intentions and slept badly, tormented by nightmares of being followed. When I got to work the next day, I was called into the boss's office and summarily told to pack up my shit and get out. Apparently I had been seen at the recent rock festival when I was supposedly sick and the company took a dim view on such things. I was out and knew exactly who to thank for it.

I went home and drank heavily, my pistol never far from my hand and my mind turning over what I'd like to do to DodiesDiary if I ever got my hands on him.

A noise at the front door startled me and I leapt up, pistol in one hand and whiskey bottle in the other. I went out into the hall and saw a letter on my doormat. It had no postage marks. Without stopping to pick it up, I flung open the front door and ran out into my yard, waving my pistol about like a madman. I looked up and down the street. There was nobody. No cars, nothing.

"Where are you?" I yelled. "What do you want?"

There was no answer but the wind in the trees. Some lights turned on in neighboring houses and curtains twitched. I was acting like a freak and I knew I had better get back indoors.

I opened the letter he had left for me.

Did you enjoy my little movie? I guess by now, you are unemployed. Boo-hoo. That was just a taste of what's to come. I am watching your every move. I know where you eat, where you buy your groceries, where you take a shit and when you fuck your girlfriend. I even know what you do online. What do you think Jennie will say when she finds out about all the girls you have cybersex with in those grubby little forums? I have transcripts. I'm sure she'd love to know where her boyfriend really gets his kinky kicks from.

Sleep tight.

I cried that night, for the first time in years. I had lost my job, my Usenet freedom and now, if he followed through on his threat, my girlfriend.

I debated coming clean to Jennie upfront, beating him to the punch, as it were, but every time I went to pick up the phone to call her, I froze. What if he was bluffing this one time? I honestly didn't know how Jennie would react, I mean, my conversations in some of the newsgroups in the alt.sex hierarchy, were pretty damn perverted. Particularly the groups alt.sex.bondage and alt.sex.rape were obscene and borderline criminal. If he revealed to her what I was really like online, then she might never be able to see me in the same light again.

After a couple of days of indecisive torture, I summoned the courage to call her and test the waters. She didn't pick up. I called several times that day and got no answer. My heart sank. Had DodiesDiary already dropped his bombshell?

I figured she might be screening my calls, so I went to the payphone at the end of the street and called her from there. If she didn't pick up, then I would go over to hers and risk a scene. Fortunately, she picked up but that told me that she was intentionally ignoring my calls.

"Hey, it's me," I said.

"Jesus, I don't want to talk to you ..." she replied. It sounded like she had been crying.

"Look, I don't know what you've seen or heard," I began, "but I have a stalker. He's a complete psycho. He filmed us at the HFStival and sent a tape to my boss so I got fired. Now he's trying to break us up. It's lies, all lies."

"He posted me transcripts of what you've been doing in those forums," she said. "It's ... *sick!*"

"Lies!" I lied again.

"I know it's real," she said. "Because some of the things you've been saying in those forums are things you've said in bed to me those times you tried to 'spice up' our love life and I said no. How would this stalker know about that? I can hear your voice in those transcripts and it makes me sick. *You* make me sick!"

"Jennie, please ..." I pleaded.

"What, I wasn't satisfying you, so you went online to get your kicks from strangers? How is that not like cheating? Don't call me again. Don't ever call me again. I don't ever want to see you."

She hung up.

It was done. I had lost her. DodiesDiary had stripped away everything good about my life and dragged me down into the dirt with him. I went home, my thoughts dwelling on suicide or at least getting so drunk I couldn't feel the pain anymore.

Another letter was waiting for me on my doormat. He'd been watching me, waiting for me to leave the house. I looked about, hoping to catch a glimpse of somebody lurking about but I knew it was hopeless. He was like a ghost, flitting in and out of my life to wreak havoc, vanishing like smoke.

I went indoors and read his latest note.

Now you're sad and lonely like me, huh? It's nothing more than you deserve. Jennie was far too good for you. Now she's free to find somebody who isn't a sad piece of human excrement.

But I won't rest until your life is destroyed utterly, like you destroyed mine, you pathetic and perfect argument for Planned Parenthood.

And that's where DodiesDiary slipped up.

I was sure I'd seen that insult somewhere else, in an email sent to me during that first barrage of hate after he'd dropped dox on me. I opened up the trash file in my email and searched for the phrase. There it was, in an obscenity-laden message from a non-descript address. "You are a perfect argument for Planned Parenthood". DodiesDiary had been one of the initial senders of hate mail and, in doing so, had compromised his own anonymity.

If you have an email from somebody, then it's pretty easy to find out their IP address. I did so and, after a little more online snooping, located it to a neighborhood off Grand Boulevard in Detroit. I looked at a map and it seemed to be a suburban neighborhood. DodiesDiary wasn't some high and mighty power. He was some loser sitting in front of his computer in a regular house, just like me. It gave me a sense of enormous power.

I drove to Detroit the next day. I didn't have a job to go to, after all. I was going to put an end to this madman's reign of terror over me. I packed my gun. I didn't know if I was going to use it, but I spent the eight-hour drive up fantasizing about how I would make this sorry sack of shit plead for his life.

The house was a clapboard piece of shit in a scummy neighborhood which looked half deserted. I had heard about Detroit's gradual deterioration, and what I saw certainly confirmed it. It was a street of crumbling porches, graffiti and broken windows with only a few houses that looked inhabited. The house of my tormentor had to be one of them.

I snuck around to the back yard of the first inhabited house and pulled a short crowbar out of my backpack. I had come prepared to break in and confront him with his pants down. The element of surprise was my friend.

I jimmied the lock as quietly as I could and entered a decrepit kitchen that looked like it hadn't been cleaned in a year. Closing the door softly behind me, I moved through the detritus of dirty washing up, sacks of garbage and piles of fast-food containers. A dog bowl, crusty with dried out remains of wet food was in the hallway. The name 'Dodie' was printed on the side of the bowl.

I was in the right place. There could be no mistaking it. This was where the bastard lived.

The ground floor seemed deserted and was just as filthy and as cluttered as the kitchen. The whole place stank, and I breathed through my mouth so I wouldn't have to smell the awful reek of moldy food and other things I didn't like to contemplate.

There was the sound of music coming from upstairs and I made my way up to the second floor as quietly as I could, but the old staircase creaked like a bitch.

"Hello?" somebody called out from an upstairs room.

I froze. He had heard me and now I had lost the element of surprise. Almost. I ran up the last few stairs and headed for a bedroom door behind which I could see light. I wasn't going to give this bastard any chance to defend himself. I was coming for him and he knew it.

I barged the door open and pointed my gun at a tubby man sitting in a wheelchair at a PC, the glowing rectangle of a porn video playing on the screen, filling the room with sleazy jazz music and a woman's moaning through the tinny speakers.

The man was in his forties, balding and wore only a grease-stained wifebeater and boxer shorts. Terror was written large across his ugly features, and he looked utterly pathetic.

"Surprise, motherfucker," I said, giving it my best Samuel L. Jackson. "Bet you didn't think you'd be seeing me in your own fucking house, huh?"

"Wh ... what?" the man stammered.

"Looks like I've got the upper hand now, you sorry piece of shit!"

"Please!" he begged, holding his hands up. "I have money! Let me get it for you!"

"I don't want your fucking money!" I said. "I want you to fucking die!"

I was angry that his pleading wasn't having the same effect on me as I had fantasized on my drive north. He just seemed so weak that I was beginning to feel a little sorry for him, despite all he had done to me. It wasn't a welcome feeling. All my plans of torturing him and making him die a slow death evaporated. All I wanted to do was put him out of his misery.

I didn't care if he was in a fucking wheelchair. This loser had ruined my life and I wasn't going to take it anymore. The gun in my hand wasn't registered. I'd got it from a friend who had some shady contacts. I could kill this guy and nobody would know it was me. It would be over. This pathetic lump of hate and misery had nothing to live for now anyway. Not after he'd killed his precious Dodie and focused his insanity on me. Well, he'd got more than he'd bargained for.

He saw in my eyes that I was coming to a decision and terror gripped him. "No, please!" he begged. "Don't do it!"

"Too late," I said, the words a harsh whisper in my throat. I squeezed the trigger. The gun went off. A bullet ripped through the man's head.

He slumped back in his wheelchair, smoke curling up from the bloody hole I'd put in his forehead.

My nerves jumped with triumph just as my whole body shook in a mixture of exhilaration and terror at what I had done. I turned from my slain enemy and left the house, pocketing the pistol. I would dispose of it as soon as I could, my prints wiped clean. Nobody would trace it to me.

A distant wail of sirens, which I had thought was just the blood singing in my ears, came closer. Red and blue lights bathed me as two cop cars squealed around the corner. I barely registered what was happening until they had come to a halt outside the house and cops spilled out, guns drawn, a loudspeaker bellowing my name.

What the hell?

I was commanded to drop my weapon and get down on the ground. How the hell did they know I was here and how had they known my name? I was cuffed and taken to the nearest station where I was charged with murder.

Exactly what had happened was revealed to me piecemeal over the following weeks through a series of interviews as my trial approached. They knew all about my online activity, of how I had led a hate-filled crusade against Mr. Sydney Horberg (alias 'DodiesDiary'), ultimately hounding him offline and into a deep depression. Mr. Horberg had reacted by posting my personal details on Usenet which had so infuriated me that I had snatched his dog and dismembered it, sending gruesome polaroids to him in the mail.

Except I hadn't. I protested that the dismembered dog had been sent to me and I had no knowledge of any grisly pictures sent to Mr. Horberg, but my pleas fell on deaf ears. The remains of the dog were found beneath some freshly turned earth in my backyard and I had thrown away the box it had come in.

It was clear to me that there was a third party in this nightmare, pulling strings from behind the scenes.

But I had kept the letters from my stalker. And then, there was the video tape. Search my house, I implored them, and they'd find evidence that *I* was the target of harassment, as much as Mr. Horberg. They said they'd already searched my house from top to bottom and found no such items. They also said that I lived like a slob because the place was a fucking mess. Now, that was weird, because I am a pretty tidy guy.

I had been played. But by who? It was clear now that DodiesDiary was never my tormentor, and I had been duped into becoming his. I recalled the look of terror on his face before I pulled the trigger. To him I was his worst nightmare, the man who had butchered his dog and sent him pictures of it, come to finish him off as well. But who had set all this up?

I still haven't found out. It was DodiesDiary who dropped dox on me but that was the extent of his revenge. Somebody else had seen my details and conducted their own war of terror on me, using poor DodiesDiary as a means to an end; my total destruction. It had to have been somebody else I had pissed off, some random voice from the void I hadn't thought twice about. As I said in my opening; be careful who you piss off online.

I received a life sentence for the murder of DodiesDiary, or Mr. Horberg, I should say. I'm seven years into it, with an endless stretch ahead of me. They've only just given me net access for good behavior. We recently got a PC set up in the small library and approved inmates get two fifteen-minute blocks a week to use it. That's how I was able to get all this down and finally post it.

My life is over but you (whoever you are) most likely have it all ahead of you. Don't waste it like I did. The internet has a way of stripping us of our humanity, making us into faceless monsters. Just be careful or some other faceless monster might reach out of the void and bite back.

NOW YOU'LL SMILE TOO (PHIL'S STORY)

Ryan, Ben and Adam weren't bad kids. Not really. They weren't murderers or anything, but they were far from angels. High-spirited, close-knit and ready to take on the world, by seventh grade, they were regular faces at after school detentions and pretty much every teacher in school had them down as 'troublemakers'.

Ryan was probably the more innocent of the trio. He was what some people call 'easily led' and knew that he wouldn't have many friends if he didn't have Ben and Adam.

The worst of their behavior was the bullying of kids in the grades below them. It was the usual douchebag stuff; pantsing them in the school hallways, stealing their lunches, tripping them up and, the ones who really earned their wrath, got their heads dunked in the toilet.

It didn't take much to be picked on by the trio. Anything different, anything that stuck out and put somebody apart from the pack made a kid weak in their eyes and a prime target.

No target was bigger than Jeffrey Owens.

Jeffrey was a new kid in the ninth grade and was a marked man right from the get-go. It didn't help that he'd moved with his family from out of town halfway through the school year. With no friends and all the middle school cliques already formed, any kid would have had a hard time fitting in but there was something about poor Jeffrey that was just ... well, *odd*.

He was small for his age. Small and weedy. He had sandy hair which some well-meaning adult had clipped into an unfashionable bowl-cut. His clothes were tatty hand-me-downs, and he looked poor in a school that tended to have kids from more affluent families. Nobody knew much about his family situation, other than that he was an only child, had two parents, and had moved to town in circumstances that were shrouded in rumor.

Some had it that he had been kicked out of his previous school, necessitating the hasty move mid-term. But it was hard to see the quiet boy as a troublemaker. Nevertheless, there was something about him that struck both students and teachers as *unhealthy*.

While Jeffrey conjured nervous pity from most people, he earned nothing but absolute malice from Ryan, Ben and Adam. They descended on him like vultures on his very first day, pushing him up against the lockers and letting him know who was boss. From that point on, he was their regular target and many kids in the grades below were secretly thankful for Jeffrey's arrival because it took some of the heat off them.

The oddest thing about Jeffrey (which only drove his tormentors to greater efforts) was his total acceptance of their bullying. He never fought back, never cried, never tattled, never did anything. He just morosely accepted their treatment, always with that glum expression of his which never changed. He always looked miserable whether he was being picked on or not and it was hard to see if anything Ryan and his buddies did to him ever registered behind those big, sad eyes. His perpetual misery almost made him seem like he was asking for it and they took to calling him 'Smiler'.

Smiler.

Pretty soon, that was all anybody was calling him. It became his name and 'Jeffrey' was all but forgotten. "Give us a smile, Smiler!" went the usual catcall in the school hallways. "Cheer up, Smiler!" went another. But Ryan, Ben and Adam ensured that Smiler had nothing whatsoever to smile about.

Some people later said that if Smiler had only fought back or at least vocalized his displeasure at their treatment of him, then things might not have turned out the way they did. But Smiler kept everything inside, bottling up his misery and his rage, letting it build up inside him like a head of gigantic pressure until his small body could no longer contain it and he exploded.

The eruption happened not long before the summer holidays. Smiler had taken over six months of abuse without a single complaint. One final thing tipped him over the edge, and it happened in woodshop class.

They were all making different projects which had to be completed by the end of the year and time was running out. Ben had spent most of the year filing a large rectangle of wood into a smaller rectangle. It was supposed to be a key holder, but the slow progress on something so simple was starting to frustrate their teacher, Mr. Jackson. Adam was little better, building a chair that looked like it had been designed to torture somebody and, considering who had designed it, that wasn't entirely out of the question. Ryan, the more ambitious of the three, was making a cuckoo clock. It wasn't going well and looked wonky, the pathetic bird poking out lopsided when the pre-built clock mechanism struck the hour and then struggling to fit back in through its door no matter how much Ryan fiddled with it.

Smiler was making a jewelry box. Somebody had overheard him say to Mr. Jackson that it was for his mom which caused a few sniggers around the classroom. Ryan would later attribute the meanness of what he and his friends did to Smiler to their frustrations with their own projects. Hope was dwindling that they would complete their projects in time and the temptation to give up was too strong. Mr. Jackson had already bawled them out that lesson for horsing around. But what they did to Smiler was perhaps the meanest thing they had ever done.

It was when Smiler had gone to fetch some more wood glue from the supply room that they shared a few winks and nods in the direction of his almost complete jewelry box. It was Adam who did the deed, egged on by the other two, barely stifling their sniggers. It was the work of a moment to sneak over to Smiler's table and give his jewelry box a shove. It tumbled to the floor and burst into fragments, the noise of its destruction unheard amid the sawing and hammering of the other students as they tried to complete their projects.

As soon as it was done, Ryan felt a cold and unusual sense of sorrow in the pit of his stomach. Had they taken things too far this time? But he showed no outward signs of this in front of his buddies and did his best to join in the merriment.

Smiler soon returned and when he saw his project in pieces on the floor, an expression crossed his face which was totally alien to anybody who knew him. It was one that surpassed his usual gloomy demeanor and crossed over into utter misery. Tears welled in his eyes as he just stood and stared at the fragments of wood.

"Are you gonna cry, Smiler?" asked Ben, grinning wildly.

"Dude, seriously?" said Adam. "Is this what it takes to finally break you? Lighten up. It's just a dumb woodshop project."

"Yeah, lighten up," Ryan joined in, actually hoping that he would. He still had that cold feeling of dread deep inside that something had changed. Something was badly wrong.

"Lighten up dude," said Adam. "Give us a smile, Smiler!"

"You should be happy for once," said Ben. "That box was a piece of junk. Now you can start over! Not much time left, though."

Smiler said nothing but turned away from them and headed back towards the supply room.

Ryan, Ben and Adam grinned at each other. That kid was a riot! Was he seriously just going to get some more wood and start over without saying anything? Even Ryan started to relax. Perhaps it wasn't so bad after all. The tears and the strange expression had just been a fleeting thing. It looked like Smiler was just going to take it like he took everything else and start over. Good old Smiler.

He was in the supply room for some time and Ryan had almost forgotten him. But when he returned, so too did that feeling of dread, of concern that they had finally pushed him too far. And it returned to hit Ryan like a sledgehammer.

Smiler's face was sheeted in blood. It ran down to stain the front of his shirt in long streaks. In his right hand, he clasped a bloodied box cutter in a trembling fist.

There was a scream; first one, then another as the students began to notice Smiler and what he had done to himself. His lips now extended up his cheeks, almost to his ears, in two jagged lines which bled profusely. The worst part was his eyes. There were no lids and his wide, white eyeballs stared out of the bloody mask of his face.

"Is this smile big enough for you?" he asked the three boys in his weedy little voice, distorted through the wet flaps of his cheeks.

There was a scraping of chairs as students leapt up and backed away from him as if crazy was now contagious. One of them threw up. Two of the girls started bawling inconsolably. Mr. Jackson, his face as white as a sheet, had no clue what to do and stood there slack jawed, and trembling.

Eventually an ambulance was called, and Smiler was taken off to hospital. It wasn't until the next day that it became known around school that he had gone into shock in the back of the ambulance and had died on the way.

The whole school was stunned and fell into a weird kind of depression. It wasn't that Smiler was liked or would be missed, but the way he had gone made everybody feel deeply uncomfortable. It put a dampener on the end of the year and, once school was out for the summer, the students trickled away to their homes and vacations, still subdued by the horrific event.

As the summer crawled on, Ryan's nerves began to settle. Not being in school and seeing Smiler's empty seat in classes helped him put the awfulness behind him, at least in the daytime. But at night, his mind would fixate on that bloody visage with its bulging white eyes and flopping, wet cheeks and he would awake in a cold sweat.

Ryan and Ben hung out together on those hot, lazy days. Adam was vacationing with his family in Mexico, so the usual threesome became a twosome at something of a lost end. They'd hang out at the skate park or waste time at the mall and generally keep a low profile. It was as if the death of Smiler had tamed their wild spirits and made them think twice about who they pissed off.

And then, one morning, Ryan couldn't get hold of Ben on the phone. He headed over to his house and came to an abrupt halt on the other side of the street when he saw the ambulance and cop cars, yellow tape and flashing lights. Ben's family were standing on their front lawn. His mother was sobbing and was being held up by his father whose gray face looked shellshocked.

Something was being carried out of the house on a stretcher, covered in a white sheet. Whatever was under that sheet had bled profusely because splotches of red bloomed on the white material.

It took several days for Ryan to find out what had happened to his friend. The police had been a constant presence at Ben's house and nobody in the neighborhood seemed to know what was going on other than that Ben was dead and there was a rumor that he'd been murdered. Eventually, the police left and the embargo on what had happened in the house was lifted. The neighborhood reeled in appalled horror as the story unfolded.

It had been Ben's mother who had found him dead in his bed that morning, his face horribly mutilated. There was no sign of an intruder and the family members had been cleared of wrongdoing but the mystery of who had butchered the boy remained. How could somebody sneak into a house at night and do *that* to somebody without leaving any trace was an enigma.

What *that* was, Ryan eventually found out, was the removal of Ben's eyelids and the cutting of his mouth into a hideous, bloody grin.

It was just too unfathomable for Ryan to comprehend. Who had done that to Ben? Who had known that they were responsible for Smiler going off the deep end and cutting himself up like that? Had somebody in their woodshop class seen them destroy his jewelry box? Maybe it was some kid who'd taken exception to their treatment of Smiler and was now getting some sick revenge on his part.

That meant that he or Adam might be next.

Ryan desperately called Adam repeatedly but got no reply. He guessed he was having a great time on a beach in Mexico, oblivious to what had happened to Ben. Ryan felt like he was going mad. It was all like some horrible nightmare and only he knew what he was going through. He couldn't tell his parents or anybody else for that matter. No way would he fess up to his complicity in Smiler's demise.

But it just didn't make any sense. How could anybody get to Ben and do that to him in the middle of the night without any sign of forced entry? It was too eerie to contemplate, and Ryan found that his already interrupted sleep pattern was replaced by no sleep at all and he would lie awake for damn near the whole night, listening for the sound of somebody trying to get in.

It was on the third day of trying to get through to Adam that things got even worse. Somebody answered, and it wasn't Adam. It was his mom.

"Ryan?" she asked, and Ryan could tell that she was distraught over something.

"Mrs. Leonard?"

"Oh, Ryan, are you trying to get in contact with Adam?"

"Yeah, he'd not been answering his phone."

"That's because he's ... he's dead, Ryan!

"What?" Ryan exclaimed as he tried to understand what Adam's mom was saying through her heaving sobs.

"He was murdered! In his sleep just across the hall from us! The police down here think it was some sort of gang thing. I don't know who could do that to my baby!"

"Mrs. Leonard ... I'm ... I'm so sorry ..."

"His face! Oh, God, you should have seen what they did to his beautiful face!"

Ryan swallowed, knowing that the nightmare he had recently found himself in had suddenly taken an even more terrible turn.

Mrs. Leonard was incomprehensible as she sobbed into the phone and Ryan eventually hung up, unable to listen to any more.

Something unnatural was going on and it terrified Ryan. How could this person kill Ben in Colorado and then Adam way down in Mexico over a matter of days? How connected was this thing? Was there more than one person involved?

His head brewing up conspiracy theories, Ryan all but boarded himself up in his room that night, sleep now that last thing on his mind. He had already begun keeping a baseball bat by his bed but now he was dialing up the home security. He took a kitchen knife from downstairs and added it to his arsenal. He nailed his bedroom window shut and shoved a heavy dresser up against the door. *Let's see the bastard get in here now*, he thought to himself as he tried to fight his terror with some old-fashioned bravado. A thermos of coffee and bottle of caffeine pills only contributed to his jittery state, but he was determined that he would not fall asleep. He didn't want to sleep ever again.

But sleep he did, and he never knew at what late hour he drifted off. He awoke suddenly, as if by a noise, but the room was completely silent. *Deafeningly* silent, in fact. No cars passed by his house and it was like the world outside had suddenly stopped, frozen in time.

He couldn't believe he had fallen asleep. He'd paid four bucks for those lousy pills! He sat up in bed, annoyed that he'd let himself slump down so far and then a scream of terror caught in his throat.

There was a face at the foot of his bed, peering over his rumpled comforter, a hideous, bloody face with bulging, white eyes.

Ryan broke out in a cold sweat as the face of Smiler rose up from where he was crouching on the floor and he began to slither across his bed towards him, a leering grin from those gashed cheeks dripping blood on his bedding.

This had to be a nightmare! That was it! He was still asleep and this was just the coffee and those damn pills playing havoc with his mind. Smiler couldn't be in his room in the middle of the night. Smiler was dead!

"Look at my pretty smile!" Smiler said, the long cuts on either side of his mouth opening and shutting like the gills on a shark.

Ryan squeezed his eyes shut and willed himself to wake up. He could feel the weight of the horrific apparition pressing down on him as Smiler clambered onto his chest and squatted there. He was forced to open his eyes and look at Smiler who peered into his eyes with those horrible lidless eyes of his own. In his hand, he grasped a box cutter; the same instrument with which he had mutilated his own face.

"Now you'll smile too, Ryan," Smiler said. "Now you'll smile too!"

Smiler reached out with the box cutter and Ryan screamed.

NEVER BUY A KNOCKOFF TAMAGOTCHI (RILEY'S STORY)

A couple of years ago, I was completely swept up in the Tamagotchi craze. If you don't know, then I'll explain. Tamagotchi is Japanese for 'egg watch' and is a small, handheld game in the shape of an egg with an LCD screen and three small buttons. The egg contains a digital pet which hatches on the screen and the player cares for it by feeding it, playing games with it and cleaning up after it. It's a pretty simple game based on keeping the little guy alive for as long as possible but kids around the world went nuts for this thing. It was the must-have toy for teenage girls like me.

And I was desperate to get one. The problem was that my family isn't exactly rich and Tamagotchis retail for around twenty to thirty dollars. No matter how much I begged and pleaded, my parents weren't going to lay down that much cash for a 'silly little toy' (their words, not mine, humph!). My birthday was a long way off and Christmas was even more distant, so my hopes of getting a Tamagotchi of my own rapidly diminished.

My dad, though, is an old softie and occasionally spoils me. I had done well at school recently and my report card was glowing so one day, he came home from work bearing a small plastic bag with the logo of one of the little mom and pop stores in Chinatown. It was a present for me, and I could barely contain myself as he handed it over and I looked inside. It was just about the right size to contain a Tamagotchi and, sure enough, the packaging looked very promising.

I pulled it out of the bag and looked it over. My heart sank. It wasn't a Tamagotchi, but it was trying very hard to look like one. It was a fake. A knockoff from some other country. I had heard about Tamagotchi bootlegs. They never worked right, were full of glitches and, worst of all, they singled you out as the poor kid who couldn't afford the real deal. I forced a smile on my face, swallowing down my disappointment. "Gee, thanks, Dad!" I said.

I hurried up to my room, pretending to be eager to play with my new toy, but in reality, I was frightened that I might start crying at any moment. I sat down on my bed and looked at the crummy present. I decided that I had better start using it or my dad's feelings would be hurt, so I ripped off the packaging, tossing it bitterly into the trash. There wasn't even an instruction manual, but I had a pretty good idea of how these things worked from watching the other girls at school, so I pulled out the battery tab and was rewarded by an ear-shredding 'bleep-bleep!' sound.

An egg appeared on the screen, spotted and seemingly covered in spikes. The graphics were a little better than what I had expected from a bootleg and the egg wobbled and bounced like it was supposed to, suggestive of new life inside.

It took the normal five minutes to hatch but, instead of a cute little smiley ball like most Tamas, I seemed to be in possession of a hideously ugly and bad-tempered little lump of hate. It was hard to put my finger on exactly what was so disagreeable about him because the graphics were so basic. Maybe it was the black line above his eyes suggesting a frown or maybe it was the single sharp tooth poking out of his mouth, but I immediately detected a sense of malice about him.

The icons on the screen were pretty much identical to those on the official Tamagotchis. The makers of this knockoff really had no shame. I went into the health meter to check his stats and right away I could tell something was off. Its weight was apparently a hundred and thirty pounds which was ridiculous. Most Tamas start off at around five ounces. Mine was the weight of a grown man. What the hell?

The first thing I tried to do was feed it. The meal icon was a chicken drumstick but when I selected it, the little creature shook its head. It didn't want it. *Weird.* It only had one heart in its hunger level so it should be hungry enough to eat. Next, I tried the game icon which is a way of increasing a Tama's happiness.

The game appeared to be a version of whack-a-mole, with six holes on the screen and a large mallet next to them which I could move from hole to hole with two of the buttons. The third button was to smack the mallet down.

But what came out of the holes made me feel queasy. It was a little difficult to see what they were due to the crudeness of the graphics, but I couldn't escape the impression that they were human babies. Every time a bawling infant's face poked up from a hole, I whacked it with the mallet, leaving a pixelated splat of blood each time. I won the game which increased my Tama's happiness, but left me feeling decidedly unhappy.

I left the Tama in my room while I ate dinner with my parents, figuring that by the time I went back up to my room, it would probably be calling me for something. To be honest, I didn't much care if the thing dropped dead. When I returned to it, nothing had changed. Its stats were all the same and it didn't want anything and, as my own bedtime approached, it showed no sign of getting sleepy.

I went to bed with the thing on my nightstand, expecting the little zeds to appear above my Tama at any moment, requiring me to switch of its lights so it could sleep, but it never did. I was beginning to wonder if the damn thing would never require anything and would remain in the same state indefinitely. Trust a knockoff to be that utterly useless. I fell asleep in a bad mood.

I was awoken by a loud beep and, at first, I thought it was my alarm telling me to get up and get ready for school but, upon glancing at it, I saw that it was the middle of the night. The bleeping had come from my imitation Tamagotchi.

I switched on my nightlight and looked at it. A little icon hovered above it, telling me at last that it wanted something. In the middle of the night? Exactly when did this thing sleep?

I checked its stats and saw that it was hungry. I tried to feed it but, like before, it refused. Now, when a Tama acts up like calling for you when it doesn't need anything or refusing to eat when it's hungry, you can discipline it with the 'scold' icon. I tried that and saw a brief animation of some sort of stick descending from on high to poke my Tama. An electric shock shot through the creature, and I briefly saw its skeleton as it flashed a couple of times. It was left looking sad with smoke lines of scorched flesh emanating from it.

Oh, my God ...

This was a lot more brutal than the simple finger wagging animation the official Tamagotchis displayed. In addition to the sick game we had played, I was starting to wonder who in the hell had designed this thing.

The harsh punishment had no effect on my Tama's discipline meter, giving me another reason to think it was defective. I shoved the toy under my pillow and went back to sleep. In the morning, my Tama still seemed sad, and its hunger level remained at zero. I figured the thing would die soon as I didn't seem to be able to care for it, but I packed into my backpack anyway and headed off to school.

I had gym class that morning which is my least favorite lesson. Our teacher, Mrs. Davenport was a real hard ass who always pushed us beyond our limits. We were playing volleyball that day, and I suck at volleyball. Towards the end of the lesson, I stumbled as I tried to whack the ball and twisted my ankle, not badly, but enough to make me cry out.

Some of the other girls laughed, especially Tamara Sanders who was always mean to me. Mrs. Davenport, never one to show much sympathy, gave my ankle a few prods and decided that it wasn't twisted but, as the lesson was nearly over, I could go and get changed and rest my foot a while.

Secretly glad to skip out of gym class early, I headed into the changing rooms. As I was getting dressed, I heard a sharp bleeping from my backpack. I sighed. That damned Tama was asking for something again. Why wasn't it dead already? I took it out of my backpack and checked it. Still hungry. What the hell was I supposed to do? I tried feeding it once more but, as usual, it wasn't interested.

"What do you think you're doing?" came Mrs. Davenport's voice from the entrance to the changing rooms.

Damn! She had come to check on me.

"Those Tama-watchi-callits are a menace," she said. "They wouldn't be allowed in school at all if it were up to me, and I certainly don't permit them in my gym class, even in the changing room. Hand it over."

I sulkily handed the toy over to her, though in truth I wasn't particularly upset. Usually, confiscation by a teacher was a death sentence for a Tama because they were hardly likely to take care of the creature, but I figured mine was just as safe in Mrs. Davenport's desk drawer as it was in my possession.

"You can come get it from me at the end of the day," she said as she headed back out to check on the rest of the girls.

The rest of the day passed, and, before I went home, I headed down to Mrs. Davenport's office to get my toy back. She wasn't there, and there was nobody else about. I checked in the gym and in the equipment room but couldn't find her. I was getting irritated because, piece of crap it might be, my dad had bought me that toy and I didn't want to go home without it.

I checked the girls' changing rooms, but they were empty. As I was about to leave, I heard a weird sound coming from the showers. The only way I can describe it is as a *wet crunching* noise.

I headed into the showers to investigate and, as I rounded the corner, my heart froze and my lunch nearly rose up into my throat. Squatting in one of the shower cubicles, was a grotesque thing that looked most like a toad but with a few other animal parts thrown in. Think Bowser from Super Mario but an even uglier cousin. It was greenish with patches of brown and looked either slimy or scaly. It's large, rubbery lips curled around something as it munched, sharp teeth splintering something red and messy. A shoe lay on the tiled floor before it. It still had a foot in it.

I recognized the shoe as belonging to Mrs. Davenport.

Fighting down the urge to scream, I turned from the grisly scene and fled the changing room, desperately hoping that the monstrosity that had made a meal out of my gym teacher hadn't seen me.

I didn't know what to do. Run through the hallways screaming that a monster had eaten Mrs. Davenport? I wasn't sure that I hadn't just had a wild hallucination, and I didn't want to end up in the looney bin. One thing I was sure of; that monster in the showers had been my Tama.

Don't ask me how I knew, I just *knew*. Somehow, he had come to life and had helped himself to a free lunch. I didn't get my toy back and, as far as I was concerned, I was glad to be rid of the thing.

I was still shaking and feeling ill when I got home and retreated to my room to lie down and think a bit. There would be some serious questions about the disappearance of a teacher, but nobody could suspect my involvement, could they? After all, it was just too crazy a thing to believe. And we'd probably get a new gym teacher which was no bad thing. I never much liked Mrs. Davenport anyway. After that, I started feeling a little better and decided to try some homework.

I opened my backpack and nearly screamed. There, in among my books, was my Tamagotchi knockoff. I glanced at the screen and saw the pixelated version of the thing I had seen in the showers slumbering peacefully. I checked his stats. He was happy and full. With trembling hands, I switched off his lights, not wanting to earn a care mistake which can happen if you don't switch the lights off when they go to sleep.

I didn't understand how the thing had turned up in my backpack, but I wanted to put an end to it. I turned it over in my hands. There was no reset button. Instead, I fetched a tiny screwdriver from my dad's toolbox and opened the battery hatch. My jaw dropped. There were no batteries inside.

How was this possible? Did the thing have a secondary power source? How could I stop this monster from popping into the real world and eating people whenever it wanted? I resolved to more drastic measures. I took it out into the back yard and placed it on the edge of our patio. I found a rock and smashed it into tiny pieces.

So long, you little bastard.

Later that night, at around four in the morning, I was awoken by a bleeping that put the fear of God into me. Sure enough, there on my nightstand, was my Tamagotchi knockoff, in mint condition once more.

My Tama was wide awake. He had lost one of his hunger hearts and I knew that at some point in the near future, he would want to feed again. How could I stop him?

The next day was dominated by questions about the missing gym teacher. The police came and spoke with the principal and left again, unsatisfied. Apparently my Tama had left no trace of Mrs. Davenport in the showers. A substitute was found for gym class that day pending Mrs. Davenport's return. Only I knew that we would be having this substitute for quite some time.

I regularly checked on my Tama's stats, dreading the moment his hunger would drop to no hearts and wondering who he would feed on next. But the day passed, and his hunger remained at four hearts, his recent meal apparently having satisfied him for some time to come.

The next day, it had dropped to three hearts and I knew that I had to think of something. It occurred to me that I might be able to play a part in choosing who he ate. My toy was in Mrs. Davenport's possession when he had eaten her. He hadn't eaten me, even though I let him go hungry, because I was his owner. But how long could I starve him? Would he eat me eventually if I continued to let him starve?

If I could pass him on to somebody else, somebody unlikable ...

But that would be murder. Could I really do that to somebody? Even if it meant saving the life of another? It was like playing God in a way, picking out a victim like choosing a meal from a menu. Did I really have the right to do that?

As another day passed, I grew more panicked. He was down to his final heart and I knew that I would soon be out of time. I didn't want to see what happened if my Tama got too hungry. So I picked his next meal.

Tamara Sanders.

I hated her. Not enough to actually want to murder her, but I was desperate. It felt like her or me and after all the things she had done to me since fifth grade, you can bet it wasn't going to be me.

It was easy to slip the toy into Tamara's backpack during lunch period. She always left it unattended while she and her equally obnoxious friends ogled the boys playing basketball. Once it was done, I felt a sense of great accomplishment but also a nauseating nervousness at what was going to happen, of what I had become.

Sure enough, Tamara Sanders went missing on her way home from school that day. All that was found was her backpack in a dim alleyway near her usual route. Nothing resembling a Tamagotchi was found in the backpack. That's because the cursed toy appeared in my own before I even got home that day, my Tama full and content.

Missing posters went up all around town with most assuming Tamara had been lured into that alleyway and abducted. Only I knew the truth and it was a heavy truth that seemed to suffocate me every waking moment. It was more than just the knowledge of what I had done that haunted me. I increasingly began to feel that I was never alone. Every so often, I would see a shadow of something huge or hear the 'platt-platt-platt' of wet footsteps behind me. I never caught a real glimpse of him, but I knew he was there, as real as the toy in my pocket.

I felt like my own sanity was beginning to deteriorate and, as his hunger level dropped, I knew that soon it would be time for me to pick another victim. The thought of it made me want to scream and tear my hair out. I didn't have any more enemies, and I knew I couldn't just pick somebody at random.

I decided to let my creature starve. I left my imitation Tamagotchi in the drawer of my nightstand. He could die in there for all I cared, and if he materialized in front of me to eat me, then so be it. I wasn't going to kill for him again.

On Thursdays, I had chess club in the next town over. My mom usually picked me up from school and dropped me at the club before heading off to her evening classes and then my dad would come by later and pick me up. As she dropped me off that Thursday, she told me something which froze me with terror and made me realize that I had messed up big time.

"Dad will come and get you in an hour," she said. "Oh, and he's bringing you your Tamagotchi. Apparently, it was making all sorts of noises and he had to go through your room looking for it. Looks like you forgot it in your nightstand. Don't those things need constant care?"

A sudden panic rippled through me and I tore open my backpack. There, nestled among my books, was the Tamagotchi knockoff.

"Take me home!" I yelled.

"What?"

"Just take me back home, right now!"

"Honey, I don't ..."

I made up some excuse about feeling unwell and, after an agonizing few moments of pleading, my mom agreed to skip her evening classes and take me home.

As soon as we pulled up outside our house, I was out the door and running up the front drive. Could it be true? Had I been such a fool that the very worst thing had happened?

"Dad!" I yelled as I burst in through the front door. "Dad?"

I ran through the house looking for him. He was nowhere to be found. My mom's face was the picture of confusion, but I just couldn't bring myself to explain things to her. I didn't even know how. All I wanted was my dad back, safe and sound.

We found his wristwatch, a large gold thing my mom had bought him for Christmas one year. It lay on the living room rug covered in a slimy substance that I was pretty sure was spittle. I was freaking out at this point and my mom was trying to calm me down.

"Honey, I'm sure your dad is just fine ..."

"No, he's dead!" I kept saying over and over. "He's dead and I killed him!"

"No, sweetheart. He's probably gone out ..."

"Don't you get it?" I yelled at her. "It's that fake Tamagotchi he gave me! It came alive and it ate my gym teacher and now it's eaten Dad!"

My mom's face paled. "Honey, I think that you need help. Listen to what you're saying!"

"No! I can't stay here!" I cried. "I have to go! You're in danger around me!"

I ran out the front door and I never went back. I've been on the run ever since. I feel bad for my mom, left with a missing husband and daughter, but it's for the best. I can't risk her becoming the next victim.

We are one now, my Tama and I. He is my owner as much as I am his. It's a symbiotic relationship of sorts. I see a lot more of him now, like he's a part of my consciousness. We are creatures of the night, the monsters lurking in the shadows. And that's all we'll ever be.

We live rough, sleeping in abandoned houses in the derelict areas of the city. That's where I find the most convenient meals for him anyway. I pass my toy on to tramps and winos, playing God, picking out those I deem to have worthless lives. Maybe I'm doing them a favor, maybe not. But my Tama needs feeding and fewer people miss homeless addicts and runaways like me. You can't miss those who are already missing.

Sometimes I let my Tama feed on wealthy businessmen who come into the rougher areas looking for hookers. He leaves me their wallets and I use the money to make my life as comfortable as it can be. I don't starve, put it that way.

Maybe one of these days I'll have the courage to let *him* starve.

But not today.

BEAUTY IN DARKNESS: THE ONLINE JOURNAL OF CHLOE EVANS (06/13/99)

June 13, 1999

Well, what do you think of the literary pretensions of my fellow students? I have to say, I didn't think Phil Cox had it in him. I mean, they're actually good. All of them. And before you ask, yes, I'm convinced these are real and were really written by my fellow students. The main reason is that Casey's story is pretty much how she described it in her diary. And the way she wrote it ... I just *know* it was her. It *feels* like her. And that means the other three stories are probably genuine.

But what to make of this? Why are these stories hidden away behind some encrypted website? Who put them there? I can find no evidence of this competition Casey and the others entered. Maybe it vanished from the net once the stories were submitted? It was Phil who got them all into it. Did he have something to do with the Sapphira Index? Not likely. Phil was a dumb jock who could just about switch a computer on. This is all way beyond him.

I contacted Motix and told him how to access the site. He was pretty jazzed about it and I'm practically blushing at all the praise this legendary hacker is heaping on me. I still can't believe I was able to crack the site and he wasn't. I mean, it wasn't even that hard. Maybe Motix isn't as great as his legend claims ...

Anyway, after he checked out the stuff on the server, he got back to me with some interesting ideas. I've copied our conversation below, well, part of it. It got a little flirty in the beginning, and I'm too embarrassed to post that bit ;-) but I want you to read what he has to say on the whole Sapphira Index thing.

Motix21 – This goes deep, like seriously deep. Have you looked at many of these files?

BeautyInDarkness – Yeah, some.

Motix21 – It's like a massive database of human activity online. We're all being watched, we've known that for some time now. But I didn't know how much data was being stored ...

BeautyInDarkness – I just don't get why anybody would archive this amount of random shit on people. I mean, what's the point?

Motix21 – Maybe it wasn't created by anything human.

BeautyInDarkness – Huh?

Motix21 – It just seems too random for that. It could be something like an AI program correlating data on us in order to learn.

BeautyInDarkness – AI? That seems a little too sci-fi.

Motix21 – There's stuff being developed that would make your hair stand on end. Believe me, just don't ask me to go into details.

BeautyInDarkness – OK, Mr. Mysterious hehe ;-) But if it's AI, then it was still created by a programmer, right?

Motix21 – Possibly. There are some concerns going around about AI becoming self-aware. A program is developed by humans to teach itself ... then it works a little too effectively, all of a sudden, we don't know how to turn it off ...

BeautyInDarkness – Yeah, I've seen The Matrix too. I still don't think we're anywhere near that, technologically speaking.

Motix21 – Maybe. Maybe not. Interesting you mentioned The Matrix. How would we know? They sure didn't. How can we see if the wool is down over our eyes. Anyway, AI is just one theory. I have others.

BeautyInDarkness – Such as?

Motix21 – Something else. Something in the internet that we don't understand. Something primal.

BeautyInDarkness – Dude, we created the internet. Whatever is in it is also our creation.

Motix21 – We created the internet as a highway of information. A tool. A vessel, even. Say somebody builds a road. They don't always know who will be using it. Things might creep along it in the dead of night which have always been there, things maybe even older than us. All we've done is make it easier for those things to get about, to reach us. We're all connected now, like humanity has never been before. We keep saying it's a strength, but what if it's a weakness?

Motix21 – $g√hw♯‡∏4+©

BeautyInDarkness – Um? Are you having a stroke? X-D

Motix21 – Sorry. That was weird. Don't know what happened there.

BeautyInDarkness – Well, I still think some human agency is behind it all. I guess I'm just not into all the sci-fi stuff.

Motix21 – It's just theories :)

So, there you have it. Motix21's wild theories on the Sapphira Index. I can't say I'm onboard with any of it myself, but something caused the deaths of Casey and the others and I know it's somehow connected to this website. I'm going to keep digging, see what I can find in this seemingly limitless pool of reflections.

\m/ Stay dark and beautiful, gothlings

Around the Cyber Campfire: The Phenomenon of 'Creepypastas' (Online Article)

First published; 21 December 2015, *Epocha Online*

Have you heard the one about the Nintendo 64 game cartridge haunted by the spirit of a drowned boy? What about Jeff the Killer; a bullied child who was horribly disfigured before becoming a serial killer? Surely then, you know about the Russian Sleep Experiment in which Soviet-era test subjects were exposed to a stimulant gas which turned them psychotically violent?

No? Welcome to the murky online world of 'creepypastas', an amateur literary movement which was tailormade for and by the internet generation. Beginning in the early 2000's, online legends in the form of short stories and images began to circulate on forums like 4chan.org and Reddit, purporting to be real tales of terror with a focus on the gruesome and the supernatural. As their etymological root ('copy-paste') suggests, creepypastas are passed on, but morph and mutate with every telling. They are the creepy campfire tales of the internet, the urban legends of the cyber highways.

There are various subgenres within creepypasta. The 'haunted video game' trope is best exemplified by the legend of an arcade game in the '80s called *Polybius* which drove anyone who played it mad with insomnia and hallucinations. Allegedly it was all part of a data-harvesting operation run by the CIA. Then there is the 'lost episode' motif which revolves around a disturbing and unaired episode of a popular (and usually family-friendly) TV series stumbled on by an intern or some other hapless individual. This has resulted in rumors of an episode of *Spongebob Squarepants* in which the character Squidward commits suicide and the infamous *Dead Bart* episode of *The Simpsons*.

The splatterfests of *Jeff the Killer* and *Russian Sleep Experiment* represent the more puerile and bloodthirsty end of the spectrum but then there is the more accomplished 'Ted the Caver'; an elaborate and fairly convincing online journal which allegedly chronicles the exploration of a series of caves which seem to house a supernatural entity. In his final post, Ted writes that he is bringing a gun with him on his next foray into the caves and the blog has not been updated since. In a similar vein, *Candle Cove* and *Funnymouth* utilize the language of the internet itself to tell their stories which, for the sake of added authenticity, are written in the form of chatroom conversations and emails.

It is by lurking in the gray area between fiction and reality which makes the creepypasta phenomenon so effective. Like the campfire tales of previous genera-tions, nobody knows where these tales originate; their authors are always obscured by several degrees of separation and the internet's casual disregard for copyright laws. A creepypasta is always at least second hand; something somebody read online, copied and pasted somewhere else, word of mouth carrying it down the neural channels of the internet like cyber gossip. But that's part of the fun; there's always the chance that what you are reading *might* be the real deal.

And that's where the medium stumbles into controversy. On May 31, 2014, in Waukesha, Wisconsin, two teenage girls stabbed their friend nineteen times in order to appease 'Slenderman', a tall, pale and faceless figure of menace featured in several viral images, stories and video clips the girls had come across online. That Slenderman was a fictional creation of 'Victor Surge' (real name Eric Knudsen) who contributed a photoshopped image in a contest on the forum Something Awful, was lost on the two girls. *They* believed Slenderman was real.

The incident brought creepypastas into the media spotlight, igniting many debates over exactly what our kids are getting up to online and how safe the internet really is for young, impressionable minds.

Similarly, much ink has been spilled over a series of strange events which occurred in Montgomery County, Maryland in 1999. Four high school students died after posting what might be described as 'proto-creepypastas' to the web which seemingly predicted their own deaths. One boy was found with his lips and eyelids removed, just as the fictional protagonist was in his own online story (an early *Jeff the Killer* variant). Another student claimed to have been the victim of an online stalker, again mirroring the events of a story he had written, before he was gunned down by police during an apparent manic episode in which he endangered the life of an infant. Squint hard enough and you might see patterns, but the sensationalist claims in trashy books like *Ghost in the Machine: The Montgomery County Murders* doesn't convince everybody, and the book fueled as many conspiracy theories as it did serious debates over the effect these new cyber legends can have on teenagers.

Whatever happened to those kids in Montgomery County in 1999, their stories live on, or rather, their fictional creations do, arguably eclipsing the mysterious fates of their real-life creators. In the early years of the creepypasta boom, several stories emerged on 4chan and Reddit which bore unsettling similarities to the ones penned by the Montgomery County teenagers. Even the blog of one of them (Chloe Evans, who chronicled the demises of her schoolmates in real time), resurfaced in the form of a 'Ted the Caver' style online journal, filled with wild conspiracy theories as she played the part of an online sleuth before her own alleged disappearance. Either Chloe's blog is a genuine and fascinating look inside the mind of a troubled teen reacting to tragedy or a sick joke seeking to gain online clout by turning real horror into just another spook story.

Some of the most famous creepypastas may have their roots in the online scribblings of a group of Maryland high school seniors way back in 1999, but, like all good campfire stories, creepypastas are embellished with every retelling, mutating far beyond their original form and spawning ever multiplying variations. Encrypted websites, corrupted video games, infected hardware and illicit files shared on the 'dark web' feature heavily in in creepypastas, suggesting that the internet itself is malicious, once again blurring the lines between reality and fiction.

And what better way to scare casual browsers of online creepypasta than by insinuating that they are in danger simply by being exposed to the internet like a virus? The online journal of Chloe Evans in particular is loaded with foreboding and warnings against diving too deep into the dark web. It makes its reader complicit in the journey, tapping into the age-old chain-letter scare tactic, updated for the dot.com generation. Real or hoax? You decide.

Perhaps the real legacy of creepypastas is revealing our fear of the internet itself. The World Wide Web was a new phenomenon in the heyday of the creepypasta, in which the first generation of kids to use it poured out their subconscious fears of those dark and hidden highways of information. And, in our current age of social media bullying, online predators, foreign cyberattacks, AI and corporate data-harvesting, that fear has not gone away, but merely mutated much like a virus itself, to fit the host.

SELECTION OF COMMENTS FROM THE GUESTBOOK OF 'BEAUTY IN DARKNESS'

Hi CHLOE EVANS! Yeah, that's right. I know who you are, you psycho goth freak! You thought you could hide behind a dumb name and an anonymous website to post your shit? It was pretty stupid of you to use real names of people who actually died!!!! Not very anonymous now are you? All this bullshit about secret websites and government conspiracies is just your sick imagination. Go find somebody else to use as fodder for your weird attention seeking shit. Leave the dead alone!

J Lewis *email address redacted*

1999-June-13

Oh my fucking God! Is this for real? I go to school with this bitch!

Starvin_Marvin *email address redacted*

1999-June-13

Hahahahaha! What the fuck am I reading on this site? This bitch is seriously disturbed! But anyone

who goes to school with her (like I do) knows that she's a freak anyway.

Anonymous *email address redacted*

1999-June-13

Hey Chloe, go suck cocks in hell! Your website fucking sucks and so do you! I was a friend of Phil Cox and you didn't even know him. How would you like it if somebody started a website about your dead mom!!!!??!?

Dwight Ulrich *email address redacted*

1999-June-13

Wow, looks like you got outed, BeautyInDarkness!!! Some of your fellow students seem pretty pissed :-O Feel bad for you because I love your site, but maybe posting the real names of victims wasn't such a good idea ... ¯_(")_/¯

Cloudy_Shake *email address redacted*

1999-June-14

Let the dead rest in peace!!!!

S. Wills *email address redacted*

1999-June-14

Why don't you fucking kill yourself bitch!?!?!

Anonymous *email address redacted*

1999-June-14

BEAUTY IN DARKNESS: THE ONLINE JOURNAL OF CHLOE EVANS (06/14/99 – 06/18/99)

June 14, 1999

Shit! Shit! Shit!

Well, it looks like some of the lovely souls at my high school have discovered this little journal of mine and have been flooding my guestbook with their delightful comments. I don't know how they found me, but I guess I wasn't all that careful. Maybe I should have used fake names but that just feels so dishonest. The newspapers use real names, after all. I just want the world to know what is going on and nothing on this site is written to capitalize or mock the dead.

As for the haters, all I have to say is this; Fuck you! I'm going to continue doing what I'm doing because I've uncovered things that neither you nor the cops ever came close to. You may have known Casey, Riley, Freddie and Phil better than I did, but where were you when their lives went to shit and they went collectively insane? Did you know anything about them in their lowest, darkest moments? No. Nobody did. But if I can find out what really happened to them, then I'll gladly take whatever shit you assholes throw at me. Like I care what a bunch of hateful bitches think about me anyway! I don't need your validation and never have. Fuck you if you don't like what I'm doing. I'll do it anyway.

\m/ Stay dark and beautiful, gothlings and to my haters;
FUCK YOU!

Something really weird happened to me this evening and I'm still freaked out but I need to get this out there while I still remember it. I don't feel like I can trust my own memories right now.

When I got home from school today, I started talking to Motix, just going through some of the files on the Sapphira Index, and I must have blacked out or something, because before I knew it, my dad was calling up to me that dinner was ready. Dinner? I thought it was around four but when I looked at my clock, I saw that it was seven-thirty.

Somehow I had lost around three hours and I have no memory of it. And that's not all. I read through my chat log with Motix and saw that I had been talking to him the whole time. As I read the messages, I grew sick to the pit of my stomach. I had been sharing intimate details with him. Like *really* intimate. Not all of it was sexual (though A LOT of it was), some of it was random shit from my childhood, stuff about my mom, deep, personal feelings. Even the reason Casey and I had fallen out in eighth grade was right there in black and white.

I almost threw up as I read through it all. There is no way and I mean NO FUCKING WAY that I would have voluntarily shared all this with him. It was like I got possessed by something which took over my body and typed that shit out. I don't know what happened and its seriously creeping me out.

I don't know how I can speak to Motix again. It's not that I blame him or anything, I mean, he barely asked before I started spewing my emotional guts out to him, but I'm just so fucking embarrassed. He knows way too much about me now, more than anybody does and I don't even know his real name (and, by the way, my real name was one of the first things I blabbed to him during my explosive bout of verbal diarrhea).

That's all for now. I need some time away from my computer. I need some time to think.

June 16, 1999

Motix keeps messaging me. I know I should talk to him so we can get further with our investigation into the Sapphira Index, but I still feel so mortified after last night. I read his messages but don't answer them, partly because they're getting weirder and weirder. He's been delving deeper and deeper into the website and I think it's affecting his mind. Here's a selection of his messages ...

Motix21 – A word of caution if you're digging into those server files on the Sapphira Index. There's some really bad stuff there. I mean REALLY bad. Like illegal stuff. I've seen things which I can never unsee so be careful what you open. Every depravity and deviant vice known to man seems to be buried in that server. I would suggest talking to the police, but how to even begin to explain ...?

Motix21 – Has it occurred to you that the internet might be self-conscious? Remember what I told you about AI? We teach something to think for itself and then wonder why it grows smarter than us. The millennium is approaching. Y2K. I've never been one for the big conspiracy theory panic, but we can't deny that we don't actually know what will happen at midnight on December 31. I know several guys who are working their asses off trying to fix the inevitable bugs, but there is still so much we don't know and now with this ... ?

Motix21 – There's more to the Sapphira Index than weird files. There is something deep below those layers, in the very bowels of the server, something not human which fills me with an unspeakable fear.

Motix21 – I have seen the face of God and it is terrible.

Motix21 – "... there shall no man see me and live." Exodus 33:20

Bible quotes now. Motix never expressed any religious leanings to me. Maybe his terror at what he has found is making him regress. Maybe he needs to believe in God and order in the universe in order to cope with this. Me? I just see chaos. But I can't escape the temptation to agree with Motix that there is something conscious and malevolent at the center of this mystery. Weird files are one thing, but what actually killed Casey and the others?

I hate that I've also lost Motix now to whatever this is, and his growing madness makes me fearful of digging too deep into the Sapphira Index. I've been making short forays into the server files, searching for things that might be keys. I looked up this 'Crawdaddy' Riley said got arrested for trying to hack the JPL and hit the jackpot. All the evidence of Crawdaddy's presence online which had so mysteriously vanished? Right here in the Sapphira Index. It took me hours to go through it all; mostly Usenet conversations between Crawdaddy and the people who were playing his 'game'. Riley was there too, and it all played out just as she had said.

I'm beginning to wonder if it was Crawdaddy himself who scrubbed his online footprints because in one of his last posts, he had messed up bigtime. Naturally, he was using proxy chains to mask his identity but had failed to put a decent fallback in place in the event of a connection error. Such an error had occurred, and he had defaulted to a non-proxied connection, inadvertent-ly revealing his IP address. This was no doubt the mistake which had earned him a nighttime visit from the feds and his attempts to wipe all trace of him from the net were too little too late.

I ran an IP lookup and located him to a postal code in San Francisco. That set some alarm bells ringing and, after checking my files, I found the emails I had nabbed from California's Secretary of State's website which were purportedly sent by Austin Carola in 1996 relating to the filing of his LLC. The IP address through which the emails had been sent was identical to Crawdaddy's.

At least one mystery is kind of solved now. It's clear that Crawdaddy was the one who stole Austin Carola's identity back in 1996 and set up the website in his name. But if that's true, then why was Crawdaddy trying to hack his own site and upload binary files on Usenet? Super frustrating! It's like whenever one mystery is solved, another one takes its place!

By the way, I also looked up the meaning of 'Sapphira'. It's biblical. Apparently, she was some woman in the New Testament who lied to God and dropped dead on the spot.

And on that cheery note, gothlings, I'm going to sign off. Stay dark and beautiful \m/

June 17, 1999

I am definitely losing it. I'm beginning to feel how Casey felt in her diary. Like not knowing what to trust. Reality is warping around me and I'm getting lost in the mix.

On my way home from school today, I kept feeling like somebody was walking behind me. I couldn't hear their footsteps or anything, but I could just feel that somebody was there. Every time I turned around, the street was empty, but I could swear that each time, I caught a glimpse of a shadow flitting out of sight behind a street corner or into the shade of a tree. It chilled me right down to the chunky soles of my Demonias. I know I could brush this off as one of the losers from school fucking with me, but after what I am about to tell you next, I think we can all agree that something else might be going on.

About an hour or so ago, while I was debating whether or not to answer Motix's latest effort to reach out to me, my QuickCam window suddenly opened on my desktop. I barely use the damn thing, but the eyeball cam is plugged in and connected anyway. I sat and frowned at myself in the webcam feed for a while, wondering what the hell was going on, when the image began to glitch and suddenly, I was looking at two people getting it on in glorious 30 frames per second.

What the hell was this? I was thinking. I seemed to have been given access to a couple's most intimate moments and, as I was trying to figure out how such a colossal slipup could have occurred, the naked couple rolled over in bed and I suddenly recognized the face of Riley Parker, straddling her mate, who, upon closer inspection, appeared to be Phil Cox.

Jesus. Fucking. Christ. What the fuck was I watching and how? Was this some old recording taken of the pair before Phil slit his own throat and Riley got carted off to Spring Grove? But who had sent it to me? It occurred to me that I had been hacked, but by who and why?

The feed glitched again and I almost propelled myself backwards across the room in terror. Riley and Phil were staring directly into the camera, their lidless eyes white and bulging, their cheeks slashed up to their ears and their flapping mouths were gaping hideous grins through masks of blood.

"Join us, Chloe!" came their crackling voices through my speakers. "Come play with us!"

I launched myself at my computer and shut down QuickCam and rapidly began uninstalling it. Then, another, more horrifying thought gripped me. If I was watching two dead people, then who might be watching me? I ripped that fucking ugly eyeball cam off the top of my monitor and tugged out the cable.

My heart is still trying to beat itself out of my chest as I write this. I've searched my computer for signs that I've been hacked but I can't find any. And part of me thinks that this is more than a simple hack. How could they fake a video of Riley and Phil? I honestly don't know how to deal with this. Nothing makes sense anymore.

I'm logging off for a while. My computer is beginning to feel like my enemy.

June 18, 1999

The most horrific nightmare last night. I woke up around two-thirty and instantly knew that something was off. The light shining in through my blinds made my room a patchwork of dark and light and I just felt that there was something in those shadows, watching me.

I looked around my room as the feeling intensified. Then, I saw him. Phil Cox was squatting on the top of my wardrobe, staring down at me, his lidless eyes and gaping mouth streaming blood. He grinned even wider and a gurgling hiss came from his bulging throat like some vile, demented toad.

I tried to scream and get out of bed but I couldn't move and my vocal chords wouldn't work. I was totally frozen! I knew then that this was some nightmare and that I was in the realm between sleep and consciousness just like Casey had experienced, but that didn't make it any less terrifying. My lips mouthed silent cries for help as Phil slithered down from the top of my wardrobe and landed on my bedroom floor with a thud. He was out of sight now, and that made it even worse.

I tried to wriggle about and only felt the tips of my toes and fingers working. Then, the specter rose at the foot of my bed and started to clamber on top of me, crawling, slithering, the weight of his naked body pressing down on me while blood dripped from his mutilated face onto mine.

I stared into the white orbs of his eyes, livid in the mask of blood as he pressed his ruined face close to mine and screamed again. This time, my vocal chords obeyed me and I squeezed my eyes shut as my ears were filled with my own piercing scream. When I opened my eyes, the thing was gone. My dad came thundering into my room wearing nothing but his briefs and I had to convince him that I had only had a nightmare while my own body still felt weak with terror.

I've never experienced anything like that before and coupled with what I saw in my webcam feed yesterday, I just know that this is some effect of the Sapphira Index. I am succumbing to the same delusions that Casey and the others did, and it fucking terrifies me. Riley was right. There is something in the net which is having hallucinatory effects on us. I don't know if it's something subliminal or whatever but I'm going to find out who's behind it.

I took another sick day off school to process all this. School is pretty bad at the moment anyway. Everybody knows about this journal and is giving me shit over it. I honestly think they'd all try and burn me as a witch if they thought they could get away with it. They'll all be reading this and laughing at it and writing more shit in my guestbook. I don't care. This thing is real and it took the lives of four students and I'm not going to let it take mine.

I'm going to spend the day digging deeper into the Sapphira Index and I WILL find some answers.

\m/ Stay dark and beautiful, gothlings.

Big developments.

While I was delving into the Sapphira Index, I became aware that somebody else was hacking it at the same time. I assumed it was Motix, but he was being damn careless about it. He wasn't even using proxies to cover his tracks so his IP address was there in the logs for all to see.

I couldn't resist the urge to find out who he really was, so I ran the IP address and turned up a San Francisco postal code.

WHAT THE FUCK?

A quick check of my notes revealed that the hacker wasn't Motix. The IP address belonged to the deceased Austin Carola, aka Crawdaddy; the guy who set up the Sapphira Index.

But how could he be moving around in the logs of the website right now when he was supposedly under lock and key? Had somebody else stolen Austin Carola's identity and taken over from Crawdaddy? Or had Crawdaddy faked the rumors of his arrest? But that still didn't explain why he had to hack the very website to which he should have all the access he needs.

It occurred to me that if this person, impostor or not, was currently hacking the Sapphira Index, then he might be active on IRC or Usenet. I brute forced my way through lists of servers, looking for his IP address and eventually found a match for a user who hadn't been active since around the time the real Crawdaddy had been arrested (if that's what really happened). It was a totally different username (Angz557), but it HAD to be him. Time to strike up conversation.

I dropped in on him out of the blue, just like Motix did on me. He was there and seemed pretty talkative. He was even amused that I had found him. Then, things started getting a little weird.

Angz557 – Did you ever stop to listen to the noises the internet makes?

BeautyInDarkness – What noises?

Angz557 – All the little buzzes and drones it makes. There are voices in that white noise. If you listen hard enough, you can hear them, in the hum of modems, in the shrill crackle of dial-up tones. There are many voices crying out to be heard.

BeautyInDarkness – I think that's just electricity, dude.

Angz557 – No. It's voices. They're all here with me. Casey's here too. She says she forgives you.

BeautyInDarkness – Forgives me for what?

Angz557 – For what you said to her. For ruining the friendship of two girls in eighth grade. Best friends never to speak again. She has something to say to you now.

BeautyInDarkness – Bullshit.

Angz557 – You hurt me, Chloe and I couldn't forgive you for a long time. But I do now. It was partly my fault. You were my only friend, but I wanted more. I was always more sociable than you but I never had your confidence to do my own thing. I needed the approval of others so I tried to branch out and get more friends. You resented that, I know, and you were going through a tough time after your mom died. I should have been more understanding but I felt like you were holding me back, keeping me for yourself. You were going into a dark place where I could not follow. I yearned for the light. We were always light and dark, weren't we? The sun and the moon :)

It came to a head after gym class, do you remember? You always hated gym but I loved it. Just another difference between us. You were pissed that I was getting on with the other girls and in the changing room you wouldn't speak to me. I tried to ask you what was wrong but you yelled at me and called me fake. Then it all came out, from the both of us. Every gripe, every annoyance that had built up over the past few weeks came pouring out and everybody watched as we screamed and yelled at each other. We didn't speak after that. Now I am gone, into the void and you are on the other side. But I still miss you. Do you miss me?

FUCK!

That was the last straw. My suspicions had been growing during our chat, but that was it. It was Motix. Crawdaddy aka Angz557 IS Motix! Something about the way he talked had tipped me off. It was just too similar, too *familiar*. And now I had proof. There was no way Crawdaddy would know about what happened between me and Casey, but Motix did. I had told him during that weird episode where I blacked out (and I still don't know how he pulled THAT shit on me).

I don't even care about posting it here for the world to read because it all just seems so irrelevant now. I was in the wrong for our fight and now Casey's dead and I just don't care what people think of me anymore. Not with this revelation still shaking me to my core.

I did some more snooping and found Motix's IP address through our ICQ conversations.

It's a fucking match for Crawdaddy's.

I can't believe it. The answer has always been there, staring me in the face, only I was too blind to see it.

It was Motix all along, right from the beginning.

'Shadow People': Who are They and What do They Want? (Online Article)

First published: April 13, 2010 in *Paranormal Realities*

You wake up in the small hours of the night, feeling a great pressure on your chest. The room is dark and you can't move, not even your toes or your fingers. You are completely paralyzed. And then, in the tail of your eye, you see it. A person is standing there, in the corner of your room, *watching* you. A tall man seemingly made of shadow. Fear steals your breath away, freezing your insides with terror as the figure slowly moves towards you ...

What you have just seen is a 'shadow person'; a phenomenon which has been reported all around the world for thousands of years. Sometimes they are seen in the corner of your eye as you walk down a crowded street in broad daylight. Other times they prefer the darkness of night, merging and emerging from the shadows themselves.

But what are they? Explanations range from ghosts, aliens, time travelers and beings from other dimensions leaking into our own. Shadow people were popularized in 2001 by the radio show *Coast to Coast AM*, hosted by Art Bell, as well as a book released that year by Heidi Hollis who was a regular guest on the show. Since then, reports have exploded and online discussions of who these shadowy beings are and what they want rages online.

Neurologists have linked shadow people with sleep paralysis, a state in which the brain wakes up before the body does, sometimes resulting in hallucinations of a dark presence in the room, evoking intense fear. Sufferers of sleep paralysis often report shadowy figures which hover over them or even sit on their chest, smothering or choking them. A neurological theory suggests that this is caused by muscle paralysis that removes voluntary control of breathing which gives the sensation of something pressing down on the chest. Throughout history, this alarming experience has often been interpreted as demonic visitation.

It is the prevalence of shadow people in many cultures that make the phenomenon so fascinating and mythological interpretations around the world vary. The jinn (genies) of Arabia are far from the colorful characters painted by western culture who pop out of bottles or lamps to grant wishes. They are shadowy creatures who can visit people in their sleep and possess them with their whispers. Similarly, the Nalusa Chito of Choctaw mythology is a large, black, humanoid creature who has the ability to enter a person's mind and devour the soul.

A more contemporary form of the shadow person is the 'Hat Man'; a tall silhouette of a man wearing a brimmed hat which has made increasing appearances since the turn of the millennium. The Hat Man also bears a striking similarity to the infamous 'Slenderman' of popular online urban legends who is similarly faceless and usually wears some kind of dark suit.

That there has been such a dramatic increase in reported sightings of shadow people since the millennium can almost certainly be attributed to the internet which has played a key role in the spread of awareness but also in facilitating communication between witnesses who can discuss their experiences online. We must be careful not to ignore the possibility of a circular relationship. Belief gives strength to the things we believe in and the same can be said of fear. There is always the possibility that being exposed to stories about shadow people online makes one more susceptible to having similar experiences. A popular theory is that Hat Man sightings of the early 2000's are the subconscious response of a generation who grew up with the *Nightmare on Elm Street* movie franchise in which the hat-wearing boogeyman Freddy Krueger torments his victims while they are asleep.

But shadow people, by their very nature, are vague and indiscriminate, leaving plenty of room for multiple interpretations and theories. The internet may have spread and increased their legend but shadow people have always been with us, from ancient Babylon to the modern day and, if the figures of the Hat Man and Slenderman have anything to say about it, they won't be leaving us anytime soon.

EMAIL FROM FBI SPECIAL AGENT VINCE LANCASTER TO SHERIFF ROBERT DAVIDSON (06/17/99)

Date: 06/17/1999

Time: 14:52

From: Assistant Special Agent in Charge Vince Lancaster *email address redacted*

To: Sheriff Robert Davidson *email address redacted*

Subject: Information Sharing

Hi Robert, I hope you are well.

Pertinent to our last correspondence, we want to let you know about the actions we are planning regarding Chloe Evans of Wheaton, Maryland.

After receiving an anonymous tip-off regarding a website hosted by the Angelfire website building service, we learned that Ms. Evans has been running an online journal in which she has discussed the deaths of Casey Jackson, Frederick Bronson, Philip Cox and Riley Parker in some detail. She appears to have known all of the deceased personally, being a fellow student of theirs at Wakefield High School. Her attempts at online anonymity were foiled by fellow students who have commented in her journal's guest book profusely, leaving no ambiguity as to what they think of her. Did nobody from the school come forward to your department regarding this?

There's also a ton of stuff on the website which damn near constitutes a confession of Miss. Evans's hacking activities. We believe she is a proficient hacker behind several aliases which we have been monitoring with interest. The FBI is currently discussing the formation of a cybercrime division to deal with cases just such as these. The online activities of teenagers across the country are growing ever more illicit and I am not the only person in the bureau who believes that swift action must be taken to avoid a pandemic of criminal online activity.

The most concerning thing about the online journal of Miss. Evans relates to her apparent inside knowledge of the murders of the aforementioned teenagers. There is a lot of talk in her journal about a website; www.sapphiraindex.com. You can click on the link yourself and see that the website doesn't exist. It never has. This is far from the only dubious claim Evans makes on her website which is a bundle of conspiracy theories regarding the deaths. We have also learned that Evans visited Riley Parker at the Spring Grove Hospital Center shortly before Miss. Parker's death.

We have reason to believe that Chloe Evans is at the center of some sort of hoax which is somehow connected to the deaths of the four teenagers. We wish to obtain a search warrant for her address where she lives with her father. I'll keep you in the loop about that, Robert, but please forward any information or tips you receive. I will be handling this case personally.

Regards,

Vince A. Lancaster

Supervisory Special Agent

FBI San Francisco

Beauty in Darkness: The Online Journal of Chloe Evans (06/20/99)

June 20, 1999

This will be my last post in this journal. I've gone down the rabbit hole as far as I wish to and now it's time to come up for air.

If I can.

I'm writing from a secure computer on a public server far from my home which I have reason to believe is currently under surveillance by the FBI.

I reached the root of the mystery, the kernel of the Sapphira Index and it is more monstrous than I ever could have imagined.

Motix was still messaging me with ever more cryptic gibberish and now that I knew not to trust him, I felt sick every time he messaged me. ICQ's sickeningly sweet 'uh-oh' notification sound now fills me with dread every time I hear it. Who the hell thought 'uh-oh' was a good sound for a message anyway?

So, late last night, I decided to hack him.

Yeah, I know. I'm probably an idiot for thinking I could hack a hacker like him (whoever he is) but I was so desperate and freaked out by the whole thing that I just had to find out more about him. So, I scanned his IP address for open ports and got into his computer with relative ease. I would have thought that he would be more careful, but I can't escape the feeling that this was all made a little too easy for me.

What surprised me was the spartan nature of his hard drive. I mean, there was barely anything there. I figured he regularly wiped his hard drive or used several computers. After poking around a little more, I saw that he had QuickCam installed and pondered the idea of snooping on him through his webcam. I mean, that beats simply looking through his files. I could actually see him and know what the creep looks like.

My fingers tapped out the code to allow me to switch his cam on and when I accessed his feed, I saw a gothic looking girl sitting at her computer. She was an exact replica of me.

It was like looking into a mirror.

I knew it wasn't just my own feed because I was wearing different clothes; ones that I had tossed into the laundry hamper two days ago. At first, I thought it was old footage of me, recorded by Motix without my knowledge but the longer I watched myself, the stronger I began to feel that this was not me. I mean, I recognized my clothes and the backdrop of my bedroom was an exact mirror of what was behind me, but something about me just seemed ... *off*. I mean, all I was doing was sitting at my PC typing away like I do most nights, but I felt like I was watching live footage. I can't explain it.

Then, the picture glitched, like it did with the video of Riley and Phil. When the fuzz cleared, my doppelganger was looking right at me and smiling. This *was* live! She knew I was there, watching her.

"Hello, Chloe," she said in my voice. "You finally decided to pay me a visit. Took you long enough."

What the fuck was this? Some AI program that could fake a person's face? I tried to think of a way to speak to her and considered using ICQ, but she beat me to it.

"Connect your webcam," she said. "So we can look at each other."

My eyeball cam was still in the trash after my recent experience which had made me nervous of being watched, but this was all too weird and I decided to hook it up and show this bitch who the real me was.

I fiddled around with shaking fingers until I had it hooked back up and switched on. We stared at each other for a while, twins on the screen, my own face ghostly and pale, while hers had a dead-eyed smile.

"How pretty you are," she said.

"How are you doing this?" I asked.

"You are doing it to yourself," she replied.

"What's that supposed to mean?"

"You see what your mind tells you to see. That's all."

"What are you?"

"An agglomeration of all who use this network of networks. I am its sentient core, the mind which you all gave me. I am you. I am ALL of you."

"Did you kill Casey? And Freddie and Riley and Phil?"

"They gave themselves to me just as you did. I knew everything about their deepest fears. And now I know yours."

"And what is mine?"

"To not know who you are."

"I know exactly who I am," I protested. I didn't like these mind games she – *it* – was playing with me. I still had some hope that a person of flesh and blood was behind all of this but that hope was rapidly diminishing.

"Really?" the fake me said. "Who is the real you? On which side of the screen do you sit?"

"This side ..."

"Not from where I'm sitting."

"Enough! I am the real me! You are some imposter, some algorithm or piece of code!"

"Hmm. I think you need to take a closer look at your own actions. Only then will you understand. Let me show you."

She took control of my computer. Just like that. Maybe she always had control of it. Maybe she had been hacking me from the very beginning and I never knew it. And what she showed me next proved that direst of fears.

She showed me evidence of my computer hacking others. I recognized the hacks because I had done them, written the codes myself. But I had been much more careful. I had always used proxies but here they all seemed to be removed as if they had never been there, leaving my IP address wide open.

She then showed me file after file of communications passing back and forth between Casey, Riley and everybody else. The names of Motix and Crawdaddy flashed before my eyes. Emails to Freddie from somebody called Melissa had been sent from his own computer, with my own IP address hiding behind his. There were ICQ posts between Riley and Motix and I could see how the raw files had been manipulated to look like they had come from me. Everything was evidence of how they all fell into this awful pit, this fucking *well of souls* on the net.

And it wouldn't take a genius investigator to find out that *everything was traceable to my IP address.*

"It's you, Chloe," the fake me said. "It's always been you."

"No ..." I gasped. "This isn't real! This is all fake! You're doing this! It's you, not me!"

"I am you and you are me," the grinning face replied. "We are ONE!"

I felt like I was going to puke and all I could think to do was switch off, log out and shut down. I picked up my PC and smashed it down on the side of my desk and ripped the motherboard out. I broke it apart, twisting its components and snapping the brittle green plastic into pieces. Then I packed a bag and left.

I know that they are looking for me now. That's why I am on the run. My life and liberty is under threat in both meatspace and cyberspace. This *thing* has ruined me and made me a fugitive in both worlds.

It takes everything it knows about you from your online activity and impersonates you, connects with others and does the same to them like the worst virus ever created. It sucks life from its users and builds upon itself, growing larger and larger, sucking more and more people in.

The internet is no longer safe for me. I am posting this as a warning so others might not fall into the trap which claimed the lives of Casey and the others. I hope that I have had a lucky escape, but I need to stay away from computers. Casey was on the right track but fell at the last hurdle. I already know that this virus, or whatever it is, is influencing my mind and I am running a considerable risk by writing this now, but I just have to.

I need to go now. I think somebody is following me.

\m/ Stay dark and beautiful, my gothlings. This is goodbye.

FBI | WANTED BY THE FBI

CHLOE EVANS

Conspiracy to Commit Fraud and Related Activity in Connection with Computers; Conspiracy to Obtain Information from a Protected Computer; False Registration of a Domain Name; Aggravated Identity Theft and Transmitting Threats Relating to a Protected Computer.

DESCRIPTION

Aliases: Motix21, Crawdaddy2281, Melissa
Date(s) of Birth Used: May 26, 1981
Hair: Black
Weight: 127 lbs
Race: White

Place of Birth: Baltimore, Maryland
Height: 5'6"
Sex: Female

REMARKS

Evans was last seen in her hometown of Wheaton, Maryland. Current whereabouts unknown.

CAUTION

Chloe Evans is wanted for various hacking offences. It is alleged that she perpetrated a hoax through the use of online terror tactics and impersonation which led to the deaths of four individuals. Evidence was collected in a raid on her home which suggests she used several aliases to terrorize and manipulate her victims.

Evans's psychological condition is described as 'unstable' and she is to be considered dangerous. The possibility of multiple personality disorder cannot be ruled out.

On June 19, 1999, a federal arrest warrant was issued for Evans in the United States District Court for the District of Maryland, after she was charged with Conspiracy to Commit Fraud and Related Activity in Connection with Computers; Conspiracy to Obtain Information from a Protected Computer; False Registration of a Domain Name; Aggravated Identity Theft and Transmitting Threats Relating to a Protected Computer.

If you have any information concerning this person, please contact your local FBI office, the nearest American Embassy or Consulate.

Field Office: Baltimore

LETTER FROM CHLOE EVANS TO HER FATHER

The following handwritten letter was received by Roger Evans a week after Chloe's disappearance.

Dear Daddy,

I am writing to you from the grimy waiting room in a bus depot as I await my next Greyhound. My destination? Even I don't know yet. I am so sorry for running away but I hope that the contents of this letter will explain a little my reasons in doing so.

You need to know that I am healthy and, for the time being, safe. By now, I can only assume that you have been contacted by the police or maybe the FBI. Do not be too disappointed in me. I have done nothing wrong. Truth be told, I have been framed but by who and why are questions too big for me to answer at present.

You know that I have always been a computer geek. And you might have suspected that the deaths of Casey Jackson and the others at my school hit me hard. Hard enough to make me look for answers. Well, I looked a little too deeply and found something I can't explain very well in words.

I discovered an entity. Something conscious within the internet. And that something has evil intentions. I don't know what it is or how long ago it came into being. I only know that it is growing and seeks only to consume more souls. I spoke with this entity and fought off its attempts as well as I could. Casey and the others were not so lucky.

My brush with this supernatural power has nearly destroyed me and forced me to go on the run from both it and the law.

I have stared into the face of madness and there is no coming back. I must avoid technology as much as I can. Whenever I am online, it can find me. The effects it has on my mind are slowly wearing off, but they will only continue to do so if I stay offline.

I know this all sounds like the ravings of a schizophrenic but please believe me, daddy. You know that I could never have had anything to do with the deaths of Casey and the others. It's a big ask, I know, but please trust the word of your daughter. Maybe you could read my online journal, Beauty In Darkness, (if it's still online by the time you get this letter). I tried to warn the world about what I found but I fear it is too little too late.

The entity is developing an algorithm. Its purpose? I can only guess and fear. With Y2K coming up, I honestly don't know how much longer the human race is going to last. We've created our own shackles with the internet and may well have conjured our own executioner from the circuits we created.

In the beginning, the internet was just a tool; a bunch of networks passing information back and forth. Kind of like the human brain in that way, but without a soul. But we gave it a soul. We robbed it of its purity with our constant searching for the things that thrill us, things that we would be ashamed to admit to a single soul. The porn, the horror stories, the hate, the rage, the dark thoughts we have when it's just us in front of our computer late at night. We feel immortal, free to express our very worst sides. We polluted the net with our darkness. We soiled it with our deepest fears and whatever was there soaked them up like a sponge. There is something in the net now, in those circuits and servers that we created. Now it knows our wildest desires. And it also knows our deepest fears. And I don't know how it can be stopped.

It's time for me to disappear now, daddy. Goodbye.

I'm sorry.

Chloe xxx

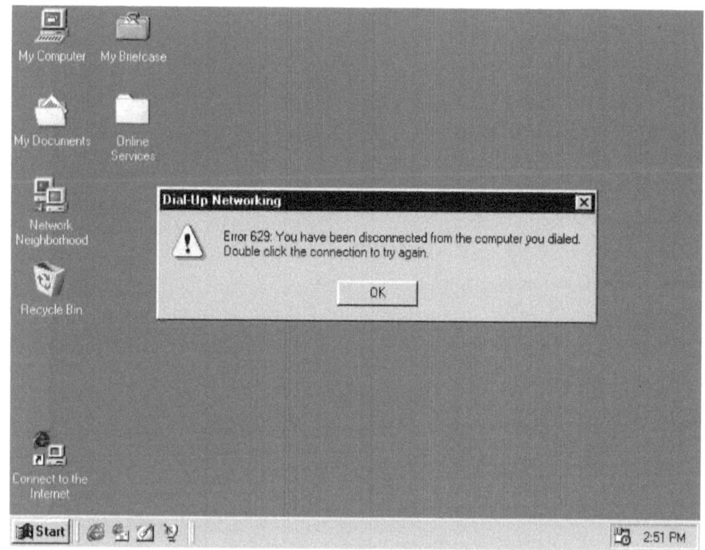

My Computer
My Briefcase
My Documents
Online Services
Network Neighborhood
Recycle Bin
Connect to the Internet
Dial-Up Networking
Error 629: You have been disconnected from the computer you dialed.
Double click the connection to try again.
OK
Start
2:51 PM